Father of the Bride

Father of the Bride

Barbara Delinsky

WHEELER
CHIVERS

This Large Print edition is published by Wheeler Publishing, Waterville, Maine USA and by BBC Audiobooks, Ltd, Bath, England.

Published in 2004 in the U.S. by arrangement with Harlequin Books S.A.

Published in 2004 in the U.K. by arrangement with Harlequin Enterprises II, B.V.

U.S. Hardcover 1-58724-657-0 (Romance)
U.K. Hardcover 0-7540-9854-0 (Chivers Large Print)
U.K. Softcover 0-7540-9855-9 (Camden Large Print)

The text of this Large Print edition is unabridged.
Other aspects of the book may vary from the original edition.

Set in 16 pt. Plantin by Al Chase.

Printed in the United States on permanent paper.

British Library Cataloguing-in-Publication Data available

ISBN 1-58724-657-0 (lg. print : hc : alk. paper)

Father of the Bride

Chapter One

Twenty-five years was a long time not to
have gone home. Russell Shaw thought about
that on Monday afternoon as his plane
winged south toward St. Louis. He had been
eighteen when he left. He had lived more of
his life away from St. Louis than in it. But
he had left part of his heart there, which
made twenty-five years a long time indeed.

The view out the plane window told him
nothing. He might well have been on his way
to Chicago or Denver or San Francisco, each
of which he had visited professionally in the
course of those twenty-five years. Despite the
brilliance of the late afternoon sun to the
west, the carpet of clouds beneath the aircraft
hid the distinguishing features that would
have branded the landscape home. But Russ
didn't need the reminder. There was no possible way he could forget where he was
headed and why. For one thing, there was a
faint ache in the part of his heart that he
thought had long since healed. For another,
there was a vague knot in his stomach — excitement, nervousness, downright fear; he
guessed a little of each. And finally, there

was the letter in his hand.

He opened it along folds that had become soft with wear over the past few weeks. The paper was white, thick and rich-feeling in keeping with the embossed DIANE SARAH BAUER at its top. The ink was blue, again with a rich feel to it, and the script was confident and feminine — rightly so for a young woman who had been raised in high society, had a good job and a fledgling business of her own and was in love with a man she adored.

Love made people confident. Russ knew. He remembered those days so long ago when he himself had been on top of the world. Love could conquer all, he'd thought then. Love could hold people together regardless of how incongruous their upbringings, how disparate their bank balances or how angry their parents were about the union.

He had learned the hard way that love couldn't do all that, but he prayed to God that Diane would fare better than he had. She certainly had more going for her. She had maturity on her side, and she had the support of her family, if he had correctly read between the lines of her letter.

We're being married at Saint Benedict's, on Saturday afternoon at two. It's going to be a big wedding. Between my grandmother's friends and my mother's friends, and Nick and my friends and Nick's family, there may be four hundred people there. But they're all wonderful. You'll like them, I know you will.

He supposed he would, at least as far as Nick's people went. He had already met Nick — once, with Diane in New York — and liked him. Nick was from a large Italian family, and though the Granatellis weren't at all impoverished, the Hill, a historic ethnic neighborhood, was a far cry from Frontenac, the finely manicured, grandly built enclave of St. Louisians of the Bauer ilk. Russ could identify with the Granatellis. He had been from the wrong side of the tracks himself. He would be able to talk with them easily.

Actually, he would be able to talk with the rest of the guests easily, too. He had come a long way since leaving St. Louis. The Connecticut private school of which he was headmaster had, in addition to its many scholarship students, a healthy share of the upper crust's sons and daughters. Russ had learned how to deal with the wealthy, and how to do it with grace. In contrast to the eighteen-year-old boy who had left St. Louis with a broken heart and a single satchel containing all his belongings, he was a man of considerable social skills. He was counting on those skills to stand him in good stead over the next five days, through the inevitable confrontation with Gertrude Hoffmann — and the inevitable one with Cynthia.

The prospect of seeing Cynthia gnawed at him. Because of that, he had thought long and hard about the wisdom of returning to St. Louis. He had a satisfying life in Connecticut. He didn't need pain from the past. Nor did he want his presence to spark anything — tension, an argument, words of resentment, however brief — that would hurt Diane. This was her time. He wanted it to be perfect for her.

For that reason, he should have stayed away. But for the same reason, he was coming. Diane had asked him to, had handwritten her request. Russ read that part of her letter for the umpteenth time:

Had Matthew been here, he would have given me away. But he died before Nick and I even reconciled. Mom has asked Matthew's brother to do the honors, and though Ray was always wonderful to me, it isn't the same. This is one of the most important days of my life. I want it to be perfect, which is why, more than anything, I want you to give me away. You're my father. I know that coming back may be difficult for you, but if you can possibly see your way clear to do it, I'd be so, so happy.

Russ believed her. In the dozen or so meetings that he'd had with Diane over the past six years — dinners, first in Boston, when she had been at Radcliffe, then in New York after her stint abroad — he had come to know her for her sincerity. While not the confrontational type, she let her feelings be known through the look in her eye, the set of her mouth, the tone of her voice. Her wariness at their first meeting had been obvious to him, as had her subsequent warming. The last few times they'd met, she had greeted him with a hug. A hug. A warm, genuine, happy-to-see-him hug.

Each time he thought of that, Russ choked up. He suspected he would walk barefoot over hot coals if Diane asked him to. Of course, she wouldn't. She had never asked a thing of him. Until now. So how could he possibly deny her this request?

The clouds had begun to thin out, breaking at spots as the plane began its descent. Russ folded the letter and replaced it in the breast pocket of his blazer, near his heart. He wasn't sure if he deserved the honor of walking Diane down the aisle; wasn't sure if he deserved Diane at all. The last time he had done anything of a practical nature for her had been when she was three months old, on a night he'd relived hundreds of times since. Having made his decision to leave St. Louis, he had bathed the baby and gotten her ready for bed. He remembered how small she was, how neatly, trustingly, she curled against him. He remembered her sweet smell, her smooth skin, the tiny noises she made as she sucked on her thumb in the crib. He remembered turning off the light and feeling himself thrust into the dark, then being caught up for a brief, bright time in Cynthia's arms, before slipping out into the deepest darkness he'd ever known.

"This is the captain again." A voice with a distinct Midwest twang filtered through the airplane. "At this time we are beginning our final descent into St. Louis. Weather conditions at Lambert Field are partly sunny, with the temperature a warm seventy-six degrees. Air traffic permitting, we should be on the ground in just about twelve minutes. I'd like to take this opportunity to thank you all for flying with us today and to wish you a pleasant stay in St. Louis."

The easygoing timbre of the man's voice snapped Russ from past to present, darkness to light, sorrow to joy — and he *was* here on a mission of joy. His daughter, his only child, was getting married. Sure, he was meeting with a former colleague, a man now teaching at Washington University. But that meeting was incidental to the occasion of Diane's wedding.

As the plane dropped lower, the knot in his stomach became more pronounced. His apprehension had nothing to do with flying, he knew, and everything to do with returning to St. Louis. He hadn't thought he would ever come back. His mother had died before he left, and his father, a wanderer in the best of circumstances, had set out for parts unknown soon after Russ joined the Army. Not that Russ would have come back to St. Louis after Vietnam even had his father remained. Memory would have made living there as much of a hell as the war had been.

So he had gone directly to Washington, D.C., where he had enrolled at Georgetown under the GI Bill. Four years later, with a history degree in his pocket, he had taken a teaching job in Connecticut and made a life for himself that was sufficiently far removed from St. Louis.

That didn't mean he hadn't thought about Cynthia, or Diane, or the life they might have had together. Particularly in those early days at Hollings, when he'd had a modest but reputable salary that would have supported them, he had thought of them often. But he had made a decision, and he couldn't go back. There was nothing to go back to. Cynthia had returned to the Hoffmann family fold and had their marriage annulled. Then she'd married Matthew Bauer, who had adopted Diane and proceeded to raise her as his own.

All that was what Russ had intended. As

clearly as he knew the words on the letter in his breast pocket, he remembered the words in another letter, one he himself had written twenty-five years before. He had agonized over every sentence, every phrase, wanting to minimize Cynthia's hurt and make her understand why he was doing what he was.

This is the only way, Cyn. If I leave, they'll take you back, and if they take you back, you'll have all the things you and the baby should have. I can't give them to you. I thought I could, but I can't. I can take two jobs and work forever and still come up short. It's not fair that you should have to live this way.

"Excuse me, sir?" the flight attendant said. "We're preparing to land. Would you raise your seat back, please?"

With an apologetic smile, Russ pressed the button to return the seat to its upright position, then looked out the window again. At the sight of the skyline coming up on the right, his heart began to thud. The Gateway Arch identified the city — he remembered the excitement when its construction was complete — but otherwise he might well have been approaching a foreign land. He had never viewed St. Louis from the air before, true. But twenty-five years of growth had dramatically altered the city as he remembered it from the ground. Tall, gleaming buildings had sprouted where low ones had once been. Some shone with glass; others were more muted with stone. Some were square, some round, some terraced, some sleek.

Russ didn't know why he should be surprised. He had been in many a cosmopolitan area over the years, and he knew that St. Louis was as cosmopolitan as any. Having been a subscriber to the *Post Dispatch* for years, he also knew the specifics of what went on inside those new buildings. Somehow, though, seeing the city now, in contrast to the way it had stood for so long in his memory, served to emphasize just how much time had passed.

He had changed, too, he knew. He had grown taller and broader. He had also come by crow's-feet at the corners of his eyes and his once dark hair was shot with strands of silver, but he wasn't ashamed of either of those things. Given that he hadn't gained an ounce since graduation from high school — and that he ran upward of thirty miles a week — he thought he'd aged well.

He knew Cynthia had. The pictures that appeared in the paper from time to time told him so. She had grown into a beautiful woman whose clothes, hair, behavior were all eminently flattering and socially correct. No doubt Gertrude Hoffmann was pleased.

15

He wondered if the old lady knew he was coming. Surely Cynthia did, since he had received a formal wedding invitation from her with his name and address written in calligraphy on the front. He had no sooner returned the reply card with his acceptance than he had received Diane's personal note asking him to give her away. He wondered what Cynthia thought of that. He wondered what *Gertrude* thought of that, the old battle-ax.

The plane touched down with a small jolt. To gather his composure he closed his eyes for a minute and conjured up an image of his home in Connecticut and the life that he found so rewarding. When the plane finally pulled up to the gate, he rose with the other passengers, took his carry-on from the overhead compartment and slowly made his way up the aisle.

The terminal was filled with welcoming committees. Families, friends, business associates, lovers — Russ's imagination touched on the possibilities as he passed by the expectant groups. Diane had offered to meet him, but he hadn't wanted her to fight through late afternoon traffic for him. Besides, he was renting a car.

Though both arguments were valid, there was another that he hadn't wanted to voice in his last letter to her. From the start he had known that returning to St. Louis would be an emotional experience for him. He wanted a little time alone to merge past with present, a little time to gather himself, because more than anything he wanted to come across as being self-assured and strong. He wanted Diane to be proud of who and what he was. He wanted Cynthia to be proud, too. He was the father of the bride — the father of a beautiful, personable, privileged bride — and it behooved him to fit the role. He had a point to prove. Based on little more than his home address, Gertrude Hoffmann had deemed him unworthy of her daughter's love years before. He was going to take pride in showing her how sadly she had underestimated his ability to rise in the world.

As had been true of the rest of the trip, his luggage came through without a hitch. So did the rental car his travel agent had reserved for him. With surprising speed he hit the interstate, intent on going straight to his hotel as he always did when he traveled, to shower away the fatigue of the flight. There wasn't any fatigue this time, though, or if there was, it was buried beneath excitement. Without quite making a conscious decision to do so, he found himself driving directly downtown, actually appreciating the traffic, which was slow enough to allow him to study his surroundings.

The Arch was as impressive as ever, as was the Old Cathedral, but those were mere jumping-off points for Market Street. He passed the Old Courthouse, which he remembered, and Kiener Mall, which he didn't. Farther on he passed the City Hall, but he didn't pull over until he reached Aloe Plaza. He had always loved the sculpted fountain there, had spent hours as a boy studying the bronze figures that commemorated the joining of the Mississippi and Missouri rivers. Male and female, they had symbolized in his mind happiness, freedom and love. He remembered spending hours sitting in sight of that fountain with Cynthia, holding her hand, watching the play of the water. He remembered touching her stomach as they sat there, feeling the tightening of her muscles, the movement of the baby inside. Given what had happened to his marriage, he should have been disillusioned watching the water's spray now, but he wasn't. Good had come out of his marriage in the form of Diane. For the sake of her existence alone, the pain had been worthwhile.

With an odd mix of reluctance and curiosity, he looked across the street toward Union Station. He'd spent his last night there in St. Louis, slouched on a hard bench, waiting to take the dawn train out of town. At the time he was sure it would prove to be the most miserable night of his life, but that was before he had suffered through basic training without sight or sound of Cynthia.

And before he'd been sent overseas.

Union Station was no longer a railroad station. Russ had kept abreast of its conversion into a complex of shops, restaurants and a hotel, and given his memories, he wasn't sorry for the change. The less there was to remind him of that sad and lonely night, the better.

Driving slowly on, he turned down one street and up another. None of the reading he'd done over the years had prepared him for so many alterations. What wasn't new was refurbished, and what wasn't refurbished had been carefully preserved. He was impressed. St. Louis had done well for itself.

He drove on a bit longer, gradually losing himself in his thoughts. He passed a restaurant that hadn't been there twenty-five years before, and one that had — not that he'd ever eaten in it. He hadn't been able to afford such places. Pizza and a movie had been his limit, but Cynthia had never minded. She'd been incredible that way. Raised with a silver spoon in her mouth, she had been willing to give it all up just to be with him. They'd be sitting in his secondhand Ford, sharing a pack of Lorna Doones and a milk shake, curled against each other in the dingy shadow of the soda shop because they couldn't go to her parents' estate or to his father's hovel, and she'd make him feel like a million bucks. He had loved her so much. *So much.*

The traffic eased. Though more than an hour remained before dusk, with the low slant of the sun and the exodus of the working set, it felt like evening. Turning west at last, Russ headed for Clayton. He had chosen to stay in the suburb for its proximity both to the university, where he would be visiting his colleague, and to Cynthia's home, where the wedding reception was being held. He had chosen the Seven Gables Inn not only for its New England connection but for its small size and its reputation for charm and warmth. He didn't think he could stand a large, impersonal hotel. Not this trip. Not when he was feeling more exposed than he had in years.

The inn proved to be brighter than the Nathaniel Hawthorne house Russ had visited in Salem. The personnel were upbeat, as well. His suite had a European flavor but was distinctly homey. A decorative headboard and footboard set off the large bed, which was covered by a quilt of a dusty blue design, picking up the color of the floral wallpaper and the café curtains. The artwork was gentle — dancers, a landscape. Cut flowers stood in a vase on a small round table, alongside a basket of fresh fruit.

After tossing his blazer on the bed, unbuttoning his shirt cuffs and turning them back, Russ picked up an apple and took a bite. Idly he ambled to the window, which overlooked the front of the inn, and opened it to let in the evening air.

Before he had taken more than a single short breath, he went very still. From behind the wheel of a pale gray Lincoln that had pulled up to the curb across the way, emerged a stunning woman. She was of average height — five foot six, Russ knew for a fact — and more slender than he remembered. What he didn't remember was the air she exuded. With the sleek linen suit she wore, the prim knot of her long, honeyed hair, the confidence of her carriage and the sober look on her face, she was all business.

Russ wished he could be, too, but the sight of Cynthia made his mouth go dry. She had been his whole world once. He had measured his days by the time he spent with her. She had been his warmth, his laughter, his hope. He had wanted nothing more in life than to take care of her and make her happy.

He hadn't done that.

Unable to move, he watched her cross the street and disappear under the awning of the inn. His heart beat loudly — the same way it had the very first time he'd set eyes on her in the soda shop twenty-six years before; the same way it had the very first time he'd taken her out, then kissed her, then touched her; the same way it had the very first time they'd made love. His heart always beat that way when he saw pictures of her in the paper, as though she were still his and simply on loan to another life for a time.

If that was so, their lives were about to collide. In a matter of minutes there was a knock on his door. Russ turned quickly and stared in its direction until the knock came again. Swallowing, he drew himself up to his full six-foot-three height, took a slow, deep, bolstering breath and went to open the door.

Chapter Two

Cyn Hoffmann and Rusty Shaw had been classmates for years, but it wasn't until late August, just prior to the start of their senior year in high school, that they looked at each other and were lost. For as long as she lived, Cynthia would remember the day she had gone into the soda shop with a group of her friends and seen him. He had been working behind the counter, fixing milk shakes and banana splits, when she ordered a lime rickey. His eyes had been brown and bottomless, his jaw straight and shadowed by the kind of beard that few of his classmates could boast. But his smile was what had done it, sending waves of awareness all the way to her toes.

She had returned to the soda shop the next afternoon, and the next. Each time she came with one less friend, until she was finally alone at the counter ordering the lime rickey she barely tasted for the excitement of being near Rusty.

He was tall and good-looking, a serious athlete, a fine student. Had he been part of her social set, she would have been drawn to him sooner. But he lived with his father in a part of town that Cyn had never stepped foot in, and he kept to himself.

That ended when he and Cyn started to talk. From the very first, they connected. If anything, their differences made the conversations they had more exciting. They became a party of two — Rusty and Cyn, Cyn and Rusty — letting other friends wander off while they talked and laughed, while they shared their thoughts, then their dreams.

The first time he kissed her, Cyn thought she would explode. She had been kissed before, but she'd never felt the heat. With Rusty, she felt it. She felt it ten times over. Simply looking at him stirred her, but when he touched his mouth to hers, everything inside her sizzled. And that was just the start. When the soda shop proved limiting, they found different places to meet, different places to park his creaky old Ford. Kisses evolved into touches that grew bolder and more intimate. Then came the day when they needed to be closer still, when her skirt was pushed up and his jeans opened. Cyn was a virgin, and Russ not much more than that, but what they lacked in experience they more than made up for in love. She felt no pain that first time, she adored him so, and each time was better, then better, until they could no more have done without making love to each other than they could have gone without air.

By the time spring arrived, marriage seemed the only acceptable course of action. They had both been admitted to college, Rusty on a basketball scholarship, and they figured that with the scholarship and a little help from Cynthia's family, they could survive.

Gertrude Hoffmann didn't see things quite that way. She had envisioned Cynthia taking the year off to make her society debut. Everyone who was anyone in St. Louis society made her debut. But a married debutante was unacceptable. *Rusty Shaw* was unacceptable. He came from nowhere, was going nowhere. He was no proper match for her daughter.

But Cyn adored him. Everything about him excited her, from his intelligence to his liberalism to the way he turned her on with just a look. He worshiped her in ways the other boys she knew were too self-centered to do. She couldn't envision a life without him. So within days of their high school graduation, young and idealistic enough to believe that Cyn's parents would come around once their marriage was fact, they eloped.

Cyn's parents didn't come around. To the contrary, they cut her off without a cent, which meant there would be neither the grand coming-out parties nor college. Cyn was quite happy to do without the debut, and while she was sorry to be missing college, she would take Russ over college any day. What did bother her was that he had to put his own college plans on hold. He couldn't support a wife on his scholarship money, and his father couldn't help them at all.

Determined to make it, they came up with a plan whereby they would both work for several years and save every spare cent. Then Russ would reapply for his scholarship and return to school part-time. It would take him longer that way, they knew, but they could make it. And they might have, if Cyn hadn't become pregnant. The baby was born nine months after their marriage. They were both eighteen at the time.

Through the months leading up to Diane's birth, then the weeks following it, they struggled to make things work. But the cards were stacked against them. Not only were they not able to make much money, but what they did make they needed to live on, which left nothing to save. Shortly before Diane's birth, Cyn had to stop working, which meant less money to pay an increasing number of bills. Their dreams grew more and more distant.

But those dreams did remain, at least in Cynthia's mind. They helped carry her through the fatigue and the worry. She clung to them, convinced that if she and Russ loved each other enough, things would get better.

Then, when Diane was three months old, Russ left and took Cynthia's dreams with him. Her grief was unspeakable. Only Diane kept her going in those first lonely days. In time, there was her mother, and then Matthew Bauer, but it was ages before Cynthia could look back on those months with Russ without starting to cry.

Now he was back, and she thought she was prepared. She had been gearing herself up for seeing him ever since his name had appeared on Diane's wedding list, and she honestly thought she was ready. She was long over the anger and hurt of his leaving, long over mourning the dreams they had shared. She had assumed she would simply see him on Saturday, with hundreds of people around to remind her of who she was and where she belonged. She had hoped to say hello to him, shake hands, even smile. Then, without so much as a twinge, turn right back to the life that had been so good to her.

She hadn't counted on his looking so tall and broad-shouldered, and so strikingly handsome that her heart constricted. She hadn't counted on the years disappearing in the space of an instant — on being yanked back to the soda shop and the moment his deep, brown eyes first met hers, then being spun ahead to that awful, awful morning when she awoke to find her world had fallen apart. She hadn't counted on feeling bereft again.

For a minute she was unable to speak. In her shock, Russ found the wherewithal to rise above his own emotional tangle. Allowing himself a trace of the pleasure that he'd always felt looking at her, he smiled. "You're looking well, Cyn, really well."

She wanted to say the same to him, but words wouldn't come. His appearance stunned her. Oh, he had been handsome — gorgeous in that tall, dark, athletic way — when they'd been younger, and the physical details weren't so different. But he had something else now. He had confidence, poise. He had presence.

But then, so did she, she reminded herself. At least, she was supposed to. She was Mrs. Matthew Bauer, chairwoman of dozens of charity events over the years, and Gertrude Hoffmann's daughter. More immediately, she was the mother of the bride, on the verge of pulling off the most elegant wedding St. Louis had seen in years. It wouldn't do for her to fall apart — or freeze up — at the sight of the father of the bride, regardless of how long it had been since she'd seen him last.

"How are you, Russ?" she said in a voice that should have been stronger. But she wasn't about to quibble. She was grateful for any voice at all.

"I'm fine."

Because it was familiar and comfortable —

and because St. Louis wasn't his home any-more — she lapsed into the role of hostess. "How was your flight?"

"Smooth."

"And the room here is all right?"

"Very nice."

She glanced at his hand. "Am I coming at a bad time?"

He lobbed the apple onto the plate by the fruit basket and wiped one palm on the other. "Nope." Then he dropped his hands and stood there, unsure of what she wanted, unsure of what *he* wanted. There was so much they could say, or so little. He didn't know which way it would go, but he did know that it wouldn't go anywhere if they stayed at the door. "Want to come in?"

What Cynthia wanted was to hightail it back to Frontenac, where the house and the gardens and the help made things safe and secure. But running wouldn't accomplish anything. She had come with a purpose. Stepping over the threshold, she let Russ close the door. When he gestured her toward a chair, though, she shook her head. She didn't think she could play at relaxing, not with Russ, not seeing him for the first time in so long.

Lips pressed together, she went to the window. Keeping her back to him, which made things easier, she said, "I feel badly about this, because I know you've come a long way, but Diane shouldn't have done what she did."

"Shouldn't have invited me to the wedding?" Russ asked.

"Shouldn't have asked you to give her away. I didn't know about it until earlier today. I told her she'd have to call you, but she said it was too late, that you were already on your way." She turned to face him. Her jaw was firm, and he caught a flare of defiance in her eyes. "If Matthew were alive, he would have walked her down the aisle. He raised her. He loved her. He was her father in all but the biological sense. Since he isn't here, his brother is filling in."

Russ didn't miss the criticism of him implicit in Cynthia's praise of Matthew. One part of him felt he deserved it; one part wanted to object. Both parts yielded to the more immediate concern. "That would be Ray. Diane mentioned you'd asked him. She didn't mention that there would be trouble if you told him I'd be here."

"Not trouble," Cynthia explained patiently. "It's a question of what's appropriate and what isn't. Matthew was here, you weren't. *Ray* was here, you weren't. For you to show up at this late date wanting to suddenly take over your fatherly duties is a little silly, don't you think?"

Once, Russ could overlook the criticism. Twice was harder. "Actually," he said, "I don't think it's silly at all. Given the circumstances, I think it makes a whole lot of sense."

"What circumstances?"

"My relationship with Diane. It's not a question of suddenly taking over my fatherly duties. We've been in touch for six years now."

"Yes," Cynthia acknowledged.

"Against your wishes?" he asked. He had often wondered about that, but he hadn't ever been able to ask. Diane made as much of a point not to discuss Cynthia as he did. It was hard enough forging a relationship between father and daughter without opening a Pandora's box of other issues.

"I knew Diane was seeing you. She's an adult. She can do what she wants."

"But you don't approve?"

"It's not my place to approve or disapprove."

"Come on, Cyn, that's a cop-out," Russ chided, but with a sad, gentle tone that took the sting from his words. "You're Diane's mother. Just because she's an adult doesn't mean you opt out of feeling where she's concerned. I'm asking whether you wanted her to see me. My guess is you didn't, since you'd already told her I was dead."

Cynthia quickly raised a hand. "I didn't tell her that. I never told her that."

"Someone did. She was sure it was true. After I contacted her the first time, she was

31

so skeptical that before she would see me again, she flew down to Washington to look for my name on the Vietnam War Memorial. Did you know that?"

Cynthia dropped her gaze to the carpeted floor. She'd known it. She couldn't have *helped* but know it. Diane had been livid. It had taken hours of talking, hours of explaining thoughts and feelings, before her daughter had calmed down. "My mother was the one who said you were dead," she told Russ now.

"But you didn't deny it."

"No."

"That was wrong."

"So Diane told me in no uncertain terms."

"Did she tell her grandmother, too?"

"In gentler terms. Diane has always been more independent of Gertrude than I was. She isn't threatened by her. They're close in some ways, but in others Diane keeps her distance. Somehow she manages to find compassion for the woman."

"I never could," Russ scoffed, "and I'll be damned if I'll do it now. How could she tell my own daughter that I was dead?"

Cynthia wished she could sound as indignant as Russ. But since she hadn't refuted the story, she wasn't much better than her mother. "It was a comfortable scenario for her. Her friends all knew about our marriage. They all knew that I'd been estranged from the family. My mother had an easier time saying you went off to war than that you'd deserted me." More dryly, she added, "No one deserts a Hoffmann. We're too valuable."

If Russ hadn't been so embroiled in his own anger, he might have heard the self-effacing note. But he'd been stewing about his alleged death for years. "Your mother hated me. From the beginning, she thought I was good for nothing. All she had to do to prove her point was to say that I ran away."

"The war was more honorable." Cynthia frowned, running through the same arguments she had that night six years before with Diane. "My mother is a proud woman. What she did and said with regard to you was more by way of saving face than anything else. She had let it be known to her friends that I'd done a stupid thing in marrying you. Once she knew I was coming back home, she wanted me to look a little less stupid. Mind you, she didn't broadcast your death around town. She didn't dare, lest she be caught in a lie by someone who knew you weren't dead at all. She just let it quietly slip when certain people asked."

"Like Diane," Russ said, tempering his anger. "Didn't she ask about me when she was little?"

Cynthia looked him in the eye. "She thought Matthew was her father. He had legally adopted her. She had his name. It wasn't until she was eight that I told her the truth."

33

"But what did you say, if not that I was dead?"

"I said you'd had to leave us. That was general enough."

But Russ knew children, particularly the intelligent kind, of which Diane had clearly been one. "Didn't she ask where I went?"

"I told her you went to war."

"But the war was over by the time she was eight."

"My mother told her you had died."

"Didn't she ask *you* about that? At her age, she'd have had all sorts of questions about death. What did you tell her?"

"I was vague. I never specifically said you were dead."

"But you didn't deny it."

With accusation in her eyes, she answered, "I wasn't in much of a position to be making denials, particularly about something coming from my mother. In case you've forgotten, I was destitute. I'd been kicked out of my house, totally disowned. The only money I had to my name was the little you'd earned. Do you know that I stayed in our apartment for a whole month after you left?" The memory brought tears to her eyes.

Russ's anger faded at the sight of those tears. "I told you to go home."

"I wanted *you*, not home!" she cried, uncaring of the emotion she displayed. Clearly he thought she had simply returned to the lap of luxury, with no harm done. He should know some of what she had suffered. "I kept hoping you'd change your mind and come back. I loved you. You loved me. I was sure we could make it if we just stuck things out long enough. Then my money ran out, and I had no choice but to crawl back to my mother."

"She didn't keep you crawling for long."

"And that's to her credit," Cynthia countered with renewed strength. "She accepted us back. She let bygones be bygones. She took care of everything at a time when I was totally shattered. If she had wanted to say you had drunk yourself to death in an alley, I'd probably have let her."

"Would you have let her say that to Diane?"

Cynthia was slower in answering. She wanted to hurt Russ because he'd hurt her, but she had never been a vengeful person. With quiet resignation, she said, "No. I wouldn't have let her say that. I couldn't have. It implied you were a bum. I wouldn't have let Diane think ill of you that way."

Russ recognized the admission as the first hint that Cynthia didn't hate him completely. "Thank you," he said, his voice as quiet as hers.

In the silence that followed, he found his eyes roaming her face, reacquainting themselves with the features he had once known so well. Her skin was smooth, as dewy as it had been when she was eighteen, and though he was sure she wore makeup, it was light and finely applied. Time hadn't changed the sculpted quality of her face. Nor had it changed the softness of her lips, the pale green of her eyes or the rich, honeyed sheen of her hair. He remembered when that hair had surrounded him, forming a veil around their kisses. Except for a few wispy bangs, it was anchored in a knot now. He wondered how long it was.

"I think —" she began, then cleared her throat and began again. "I think I'll sit down after all." Her knees weren't as steady as she wanted them to be — Russ's scrutiny had always done that to her — and there was still the matter of the wedding to decide. Slipping into the chair that he had offered her earlier, she crossed her legs, folded her hands in her lap and looked up with what she hoped was restored composure. "About your relationship with Diane —"

"I'm not giving her up," Russ vowed. "I'm not walking away. I did that once, because I felt I had no choice, but I can't do it again. She's my daughter. Anyone looking at the two of us together can see that."

Cynthia would be the last one to argue. She remembered how painful it had been, particularly in those first hard years, to look at Diane and see the resemblance. In time that resemblance took a back seat to Diane's vibrant personality. Still, there were odd moments when a look or a gesture would conjure up Russ again.

"I've never denied that she was your daughter, and I'm not asking you to give her up. I'm simply asking that you let my brother-in-law walk her down the aisle."

"Why is that so important to you?"

"Diane has always been close to him — and to his daughter, Lisa, who's the maid of honor. Ray was good to us over the years, particularly after Matthew died. I felt it was an honor he should be given. Besides, I've already asked him. To take back the invitation would be a slap in the face."

"Not if you explained the situation."

"I'd rather not do that."

"Explain the situation? Or take back the invitation?"

"Either."

Russ sank into the chair opposite her. He sat forward with his elbows on his knees and laced his fingers in the gap between. "I can buy the problem about taking back the invitation. But I'm not sure I understand why explaining the situation is so difficult. If Ray is fond of Diane, he should want what she wants." An unpleasant idea intruded on that thought. "Are you dating him?"

"Of course not. He's my brother-in-law, and he's married."

"Are you dating someone else?"

"I don't think that's relevant here."

Russ knew it wasn't, but since he had broached the topic, he wasn't backing down. He wanted to know what to expect on Saturday. "I'm curious."

"You gave up your right to curiosity the night you walked out on me," Cynthia said more sharply than she'd planned. Seeing Russ had stirred up old feelings, the most immediate of which was anger at his desertion. She hadn't realized the feeling was still so strong.

He turned his hands over and studied them. In a grim voice, he said, "I didn't walk out on you. Not the way you make it sound."

"You left. I had a three-month-old baby, a one-room apartment with someone else's furnishings in it and two hundred dollars in my bag."

"That was more than I had." He had taken only the train fare, wanting to leave everything else for her.

"But I couldn't work. You could. You were supposed to take care of me."

"On *what?*" He raised his eyes. "I had a high school diploma and no skills. I was working two jobs, neither of which would get me to first base, and when I wasn't working, I was helping you with the baby. I was exhausted and scared and disgusted with myself that I couldn't do better. So I left. You can criticize me for that, but it wasn't a decision I made lightly. I agonized. I went through the alternatives again and again, trying to find a way to make it work. But it was a vicious circle. Without a college education, I couldn't earn good money, but I couldn't get the college education because I wasn't earning good enough money to stop working and study." He raked a hand through his hair. "Don't you think I wanted to stay? I adored the baby, and you — you were the light of my life! I wanted to give you so much, but I wasn't going to be able to give you a damn thing the way we were going. All I was doing was sentencing you to a life of hard labor. That tore me apart. So I sent you back home."

"Without asking whether I wanted to go," Cynthia challenged, but the challenge fizzled with Russ's immediate acknowledgment.

"Of course you didn't want to go. I knew that. I knew that as long as I hung around, you'd be right there with me. But your mother wouldn't accept me, and because of that, she wouldn't accept you or the baby. And because of that, you were suffering in ways you didn't deserve. We were living in poverty, for God's sake."

"I didn't think it was so bad."

"You would have after a year, or two or three. You would have thought back to what you'd grown up with and begun to wonder where you were going. You'd have hated me by then."

"No —"

"Yes." He was determined to make her understand why he had left her that fateful night. "I saw it happen with my parents. My mother kept thinking things would get better, but they never did. Poverty eats at relationships like nothing else can. By the time she died, she couldn't stand the sight of my father."

"But we loved each other!"

"So did my parents when they first married. I thought our situation was different because of your family. I thought that if I could support myself with my scholarship and they could support you until I graduated, we'd do fine. I assumed too much."

"We both assumed it," Cynthia argued. She didn't like Russ playing the martyr, when they had made their decisions together.

"Well, we assumed wrong. We were bucking the tide, Cyn. There was no way we were going to keep from drowning at the rate we were going. I was dragging you under. I had to leave."

"So you disappeared."

He let out a breath and sat back. "I joined the army. It was the only thing I could afford."

"You never wrote me."

"I figured you were back home and that

there would only be trouble if mail arrived from me."

He was right, she knew, but she wasn't conceding the point aloud. For years she had been haunted by the fact that he had never tried to contact her after he'd gone. "You could have written to Diane."

"She was too young to read, and by the time she was old enough, you were married to Bauer."

"You could have written to her then. You could have contacted her. You could have let her know that her father cared."

"Would that have made life easier for her?"

"Yes!" Cynthia exclaimed, but the expression on her face that followed gave her away.

"It wouldn't have," Russ chided. "She had a wonderful life. She had you and Bauer. She had dancing lessons and private school and big birthday parties on the lawn of your home. She even had a horse of her own."

"You didn't know that then."

"I did. The Bauers were society. The *Post Dispatch* covered most everything you did."

"You read the *Post Dispatch*?" she asked in surprise. She knew he'd been living in Connecticut for years. She couldn't believe that the *Post Dispatch* was sold on newsstands there.

"I've subscribed to the thing since the day I was discharged from the army. It was the only way I could keep up with what you were doing."

Cynthia felt a small ache in the pit of her stomach. For years she'd assumed that Russ had pushed her into his past and gone on with his life. Believing that had made it easier for her to do the same. Now, knowing that he'd never forgotten her, she felt a rush of things that spelled trouble. To ward it off, she ignored his statement. Rather, out of sheer curiosity, she asked, "What made you finally contact Diane?"

"I read about her graduation from high school and knew she was going to Radcliffe. College seemed the right time to contact her."

"When she was away from me?"

Cynthia had always been quick. That was one of the things Russ had loved about her. She hadn't played sweet and dumb, like the other girls. She put two and two together, often guessing his thoughts before he expressed them. Apparently she hadn't changed.

"I didn't know what you'd told her," he explained. "I didn't know how you felt about me yourself. It seemed easier to wait until she was out of the house. That way I wouldn't have to deal with your feelings, too."

"But you waited until her sophomore year."

"Freshman year is tough for kids, with all that's new and different. I wanted to give her a chance to settle in and realize she wasn't going to flunk out before I threw her a major loop." He arched a brow. "Aside from not believing me, she wasn't terribly thrown."

"She has a level head on her shoulders." *She got that from you,* Cynthia wanted to say, but resisted.

"She's a great girl. You did a good job, Cyn."

The compliment was from the heart. Cynthia sensed that, and it touched her more than she wanted to be touched. Lowering her eyes, she twisted the ring on her finger. Actually, there were three rings, two simple gold bands flanking a central one studded with diamonds and sapphires — wedding bands and an engagement ring that Matthew had given her. Looking at them reminded her who had helped raise Diane into the great girl she was.

Eyes still lowered, she said, "I would really prefer to have Ray give her away."

Russ had felt she was beginning to soften and was immediately disappointed. "If you're ashamed of me," he burst out, leaning forward again, "there's no need. I have a Ph.D., a prestigious position and a fine reputation. I know how to talk, how to act, even how to waltz. I've already made arrangements with the shop Nick is using to be fitted for a morning coat, striped pants and the rest tomorrow, so I'll look as dignified as any man there, and if it's a matter of the amount of money in my bank account —"

"That's not it," she cut in.

"Then what is? Is Ray particularly fragile?"

"Not at all."

His eyes hardened. "Then it is me. My existence. That's it, isn't it? You have your place in society, and you don't want it threatened. You don't want people reminded that you married beneath yourself and that Diane's father deserted her. There'll be people there who don't know I ever existed, and you want to keep it that way."

"That's not it!" she cried. But her composure was starting to crumble — not so much because of what he was saying as because of the look in his eyes. The hardness was new. He had never looked at her that way before. In the past there had been nothing but gentleness, understanding and adoration. Irrational though it was, given that they were nothing to each other anymore, what she saw now hurt her nearly as much as his disappearance had twenty-five years before.

Rising to her feet with a surge of feeling, she cried, "It's me. *Me*. Seeing you hurts *me!* I've spent months planning every detail of this wedding because I want the day to be perfect, so I've been excited, but tense, too. When Diane put your name on her list, I knew I'd have trouble, but I told myself I could handle it. I'm grown-up. I'm rational. I'm past pettiness." She shook her head. "But your walking her down the aisle is too much."

"I'm her *father,* for God's sake, and a wedding is a milestone."

"So is going off to kindergarten, but were you there for that? Or for her first horse show? Or her first ballet recital?"

"I couldn't be there then," he said more quietly as he looked up at her. "I've already told you why."

But Cynthia wasn't thinking of his reasons. She was reliving the agony of losing him. "You weren't there when I ran out of money. You weren't there when I knew what I had to do but was terrified of doing it. You weren't there when I thought I was pregnant again."

The air was still. "Pregnant?"

"Yes, pregnant."

"With another baby of *ours?*"

"Who else's baby would I have had?" she cried. "All the signs were there. I was sure I was pregnant. I didn't know whether to be happy or sad, so all I was was scared to death!"

In hindsight, Russ felt all those things for her, plus a helplessness in the here and now. "I didn't know."

"Of course you didn't know. You were too busy playing soldier and convincing yourself that you'd done the honorable thing."

His eyes went wide in disbelief. "Playing

soldier? I was *miserable*."

"But you didn't come back!"

"I couldn't!"

"But I needed you!"

Hearing the words, seeing the look in her eyes that said she had felt betrayed, Russ understood that this airing of their emotions had been inevitable. But they were going in circles, and it was painful. He didn't know how much more he could take.

Cynthia was wondering the very same thing about herself. She hadn't planned to fall apart. It was fine to say that she'd been under pressure of late, but that didn't excuse what she was doing or saying. There was no point in lashing out about what was long since over and done.

"About the wedding," she began with a sigh, only to stop when he rose abruptly from his chair and crossed to the bed. The muscles of his shoulders flexed when he reached into the blazer that lay there. Her gaze fell to his pants, stylish twill ones that broadcast the tightness of his bottom and the length of his legs. She had always loved those legs — strong and well formed without being grossly muscular, and, though hairy, not so much a thick, wiry kind of hair as a wispier, smoother kind. She remembered sitting naked beside him, running her hands up and down those legs —

"Before you say anything else about the

wedding, Cyn, I think you should read this."

Her eyes shot to the folded paper he held. She took it and lowered it to her lap, which gave her the excuse to drop her head, the only way she could hide the color she was sure stained her cheeks. The feel of the paper was familiar. Even before she opened it and saw the name embossed at the top, she knew it to be a piece of the stationery she had ordered for Diane six months before, at the same time she'd ordered the wedding invitations that had long since been mailed.

She read the entire letter. It was a chatty one, telling Russ in the lightest tone, almost tongue in cheek, about the parties and dinners of the past few months, then about plans for the wedding itself. The tone grew introspective when she related her feelings for Nick, her excitement about the marriage, her hopes for the future. The tone grew softer and more beseeching when she asked Russ to give her away.

Without raising her eyes, Cynthia held the letter for a minute longer before refolding it. She knew why Russ had let her read it. More than anything he might have said, it spoke of the relationship that had grown between Diane and him in the past six years. It made another point, too, one that was directly relevant to the issue of the wedding. Diane had asked Russ to walk her down the aisle. The idea had come from her. Clearly it was something Diane very much wanted.

The fact that Cynthia didn't want it was suddenly irrelevant. So much of what she had done in life — including returning to her mother's after Russ had left — had been done for Diane. Given her druthers, Cynthia would probably have gone off in search of him. But Diane had needed care and protection, and Cynthia had been determined to give her both. She loved her daughter. She wanted her to be happy. That would never change.

She passed the letter back to Russ, but for a moment she didn't let go. Quietly, thoughtfully, with her eyes focused on the spot where his large hand closed over the paper, she said, "When Diane was little, I spoiled her terribly. She was so undemanding, it was easy to do that. She rarely asked for anything she didn't really want, and when I gave her whatever it was, she thanked me forever. Despite all she had growing up, she never took things for granted. I know she couldn't possibly have remembered how strapped we were during the first three months of her life, but there were times when I wondered whether it somehow registered on her subconscious."

Dropping her hand from the letter, she dared raised her eyes for a final moment. "I'll talk with Ray," she said. Without another word, she left the room.

Chapter Three

By the time Russ arrived at the Bauer home at nine-thirty the next morning, he was already well into his day. He had awoken at six, taken a forty-minute run along a course that the hotel management had recommended, and returned to shower. After putting down a full breakfast at Bernard's, a restaurant at the inn, he set off in the car to see those things he hadn't seen the day before — namely, the neighborhood where he'd grown up.

He found a mixed bag. The schools he had gone to looked exactly as he remembered them, as did the library and the supermarket, but the soda shop had been converted into a video store, and the house he had called home had been razed.

Cruising down one street and up another, his eyes darting left to right in recognition of familiar landmarks, he gathered memories. Some were of the days before he had met Cyn; most were of the days after. They had had such good times together. The simple act of walking down a street with her had been a joy. He remembered the way she had leaned into him, wrapped her arm around his waist, matched her step to his. Mostly he remembered the way she had looked up at him with happy, trusting eyes. She had made him feel invincible, a grave error on his part. If he had been more realistic, he might have been able to prevent the pain.

Hundreds of times he had wondered what would have happened if he and Cynthia had known before they eloped what Cynthia's mother would do. He supposed they would have waited, gone to college, stolen time together. He supposed that when he finally got his degree and was gainfully employed, when he'd finally been able to support Cynthia without Gertrude's help, they would have married. Then again, in the ensuing years Cynthia might have been swept up into the whirl of society and left him behind. That thought had terrified him.

The irony of it, he realized as he headed for Frontenac, was that that early fear had come to pass with Cynthia's marriage to Matthew Bauer. In addition to being older, Bauer had been everything Russ wasn't. He'd been educated. Cultured. Wealthy. He'd been a perfect match for Cynthia, as society matches went. Had he made her happy?

If happiness was judged by the beauty of one's home, the answer had to be yes. Russ had known the Bauers lived in an elegant area, but he wasn't quite prepared for the extent of the elegance when he turned onto their street and found their drive. It was flanked by two brick gateposts covered with ivy, as was the gatekeeper's cottage just inside. Since the black wrought-iron gates were open, he passed through and proceeded slowly up the drive.

That slow procession was an education in and of itself. The drive was pebbled, perfectly edged and newly replenished, if the light gray of the stones was any indication. Lush green lawns rolled away from the drive on either side, ending in a stand of maples and birches on the left and an apple orchard on the right. Ahead was a collection of trees and shrubs that he was sure a landscape architect had been paid a bundle to create. Likewise, he was sure, the upkeep cost a bundle. Russ could see no fewer than three gardeners working — one mowing the lawn in the distance, two others trimming the greenery in front of the house.

The house itself was brick and ivy-covered, as the gatekeeper's had been, but that was where the similarity ended. This one was Georgian and large, with no fewer than twenty windows blinking back those rays of the sun that made it through the trees.

Russ lived in an area where ivy-covered brick was common. His own house had its share. But his own house was modest compared to this one — not that anything here was gaudy, he had to admit. It was impeccably kept, from the neatly painted black gutters to the shiny black shutters to the clean, bluestone walk and the polished brass numbers on one of the front columns. The house was clearly ready for a wedding. Russ felt good for Diane. And for Cynthia.

The drive branched to form a circle before the front door. Russ pulled to the right, parked halfway around and turned off the ignition. He had told Diane he would be there, so he was, though he had second thoughts about the visit. The words that had passed between Cynthia and him were still fresh and stinging. He wished he had had time to put them into perspective.

Diane. Think of Diane. She's all that matters this week, he told himself. Still, it was Cynthia he thought of as he climbed from the car and approached the house. He wondered whether Bauer had owned the place before she met him, whether she had lent a hand in shaping the landscaping, whether she remembered that she and Russ had always talked about owning a place in the woods.

The brass knocker was as polished as the numbers. He rapped twice, then waited. After a minute the door was opened by a young black woman, who, wearing a simple linen sheath, low heels and pearls, was as elegant as the house.

"Dr. Shaw?" she asked, then stood back

with a smile to gesture him in. "Of course you're Dr. Shaw. The resemblance between you and Diane is marked." She extended her hand. "Diane told me you were coming. I'm Mandy Johnson, Mrs. Bauer's social secretary."

"Social secretary," Russ echoed, shaking the woman's hand. He had assumed a housekeeper, a cook and cleaning people, but not a social secretary.

"Actually," Mandy explained, "I'm here to help out with the wedding. Usually I work for Mrs. Hoffmann."

Russ found that even more surprising. His limited experience with Gertrude Hoffmann had taught him she was something of a bigot. If the young woman before him was for real, he was impressed. He was about to ask how long she had worked for Gertrude when a shout drew his attention to the top of the winding stairs.

"Russ!"

Diane came trotting down, ran to him and threw her arms around his neck. He hugged her tightly for a minute, then held her back for a speculative once-over. From the crown of her straight, dark blond hair to the tips of her white ballet flats, she was a beauty. His gaze lingered on her sundress. He recognized the pattern as a staple among girls at his school. "Laura Ashley?" he teased.

She laughed. "I know, I know. Totally out

of character. If I were in New York, I'd be wearing either jeans or silk, but this is St. Louis, and St. Louis is Grandmother's turf. I'm going over to see her later."

"Ah," Russ said sagely. Mandy Johnson had quietly disappeared, leaving Diane and him alone. "You look great, Laura Ashley and all."

She grinned. "Thanks. You, too. I like the shirt. I've never seen you in anything but a tie and jacket before."

He was wearing a soft, oversize white jersey, tucked into a pair of snug-fitting chinos, and deck shoes without socks. "Even stuffy old professors have to relax sometimes."

"Stuffy?" she asked dubiously, and followed it up with a mocking "*Old?* If you looked any younger, they'd never believe you were my father."

"I was a child dad."

Chuckling, she gave him a final squeeze before releasing her hold on his neck. "Want some breakfast?"

"Already had some."

"How about coffee?"

"Yeah, that'd be nice — but only if it's made."

Slipping her arm through his, she guided him through the front hall and down a side corridor. "It's always made around here. Mrs. Fritz sees to that."

"Mrs. Fritz is the cook, I take it?"

"You take right." They entered the kitchen, where a small, round woman was kneading what Russ guessed to be bread dough. "Mrs. Fritz, say hello to Dr. Shaw."

The cook scowled. In a voice heavy with German intonation, she said, "How do you do, Dr. Shaw. I must make excuses for Miss Bauer once again. I have told her many, many times not to bring her guests through the kitchen. If you would like something to eat, I will be glad to serve you in the dining room."

Undaunted by the woman's reprimand, Diane dropped Russ's arm and made for the coffee maker. "No need to wait on us. We're just having coffee. You make a great cup, Mrs. Fritz." She filled two mugs with the dark brew — remembering that Russ took his black — and motioned him toward a side, screened door. Moments later she was placing the mugs on the table and settling into a white, cushioned wicker chair.

"Beautiful setting," Russ observed. The patio was of flagstone and huge. In addition to the six chairs at the table, there were occasional wicker armchairs and lounges scattered among large potted plants. Beds of brightly colored flowers bordered the flagstone, broken only by broad stone steps that led to the lawn. Set into one side of that lawn was a gleaming turquoise pool. Balancing it on the other side was a rose garden in vivid red bloom. The remainder of the lawn was an expanse of lavish green, undulating gently into the distance, where a gazebo fronted a graceful grove of willows.

"Take a good look," Diane said with a sigh. "This is the last time you'll see it like this for a while. The tent people start bringing things tomorrow. By the time they've set up fifty-plus tables, four hundred chairs and a dance floor, the place won't look half as peaceful."

"It'll still be spectacular." He took his eyes from the view to study Diane. "How's Nick?"

She grinned. "Great."

"Are you excited?"

"Very. And nervous. There are so many things to think about. Mandy has been a godsend. So has Tammy — she's a party planner and, boy, she's earned her money with this one. If it isn't the caterer on the phone, it's the florist or the photographer or the videographer or the dressmaker or the jeweler or the stationer. I swear, if I'd realized what was involved with an extravaganza like this, I would have eloped. Up until the very day the invitations went out, I was considering it. If it hadn't been for my grandmother . . ." Her voice trailed off.

Russ raised the mug to his mouth and took a drink. The brew was satisfying — Diane had been right about that — but the true satisfaction came with the company. Having spent so many years alone and out of touch, he was stunned each time he saw her to realize Diane was his. "You're doing this for Gertrude, then?"

"In part. She loves productions." Diane sent him an apologetic look. "I know you never had cause to feel kindly toward her, but she's mellowed over the years. In some regards, she's a lonely old lady. She has lots of friends, but at the end of each day she has no one to go home to but the hired help. It's sad."

Russ couldn't feel too badly for the woman. "I'm surprised she doesn't live here with your mother and you."

Diane nearly choked on her coffee. With a hand on her chest, she said, "Are you kidding? I may have said she's mellowed, but that doesn't mean she's a peach. If she were here, she'd be driving everyone crazy. As it is, she's going to antagonize the photographer and the videographer when she insists they be hidden behind flowers and latticework at the wedding ceremony." She snorted. "I really *should* have eloped."

"No," Russ said. "That wouldn't have been right."

"You did."

"We had no other choice. If we'd told your grandmother what we wanted to do, she wouldn't have allowed us to get married at all. Then we wouldn't have had you, and that would have been awful."

Diane stared at him for a minute before breaking into the gentlest, sincerest of smiles. "I'm so glad you're here. I don't care if she's furious —"

"Your mother?"

"My grandmother."

"Is your mother angry?" Russ was anxious to know. He wondered how much of her feelings Cynthia shared with Diane.

"She was yesterday afternoon. She was quieter when she came in last night." Diane dropped her gaze to her coffee. "I'm sorry about that. I didn't think she'd actually go over to see you. Was it very uncomfortable?"

"Not as bad as it might have been. Was *she* uncomfortable?"

"A little, I think." Her eyes returned to his. "That's why it's good you came on Monday. She has the whole week to get used to seeing you so she doesn't start to hyperventilate on the day of the wedding."

"Hyperventilate?" he quipped. "Your mother?" Cool, composed Cynthia Hoffmann? It was an intriguing thought. "Why in the world would she hyperventilate?"

"Because you're handsome enough in a shirt and chinos or a blazer and tie. In formal wear you'll be a killer."

Russ grinned. "Are all daughters good for

their fathers' egos, or is mine just unusually biased?"

"Maybe I'm making up for lost time," she said with a softness that brought a lump to his throat.

He curved a hand around her neck. "You and me both." Leaning forward, he kissed her cheek. He barely had time to draw back when Diane's gaze shot past him. He caught looks of surprise, then pleasure, then unsureness on her face before he glanced around.

Cynthia had just come past the side of the house. The sight of her brought him to his feet and at the same time took his breath away. She had been running — at least that was what it looked like to Russ, who had run with enough people over the years to recognize the symptoms. Though she was standing stock-still now, she was breathing hard. She wore top-of-the-line running shoes that looked well used, a pair of brief, teal green nylon shorts and a matching singlet. Her hair cascaded from a high ponytail, from which had escaped loose, honey-colored wisps. Along with her bangs, they framed her face, several catching in the rivulets of sweat that trickled down her cheeks. Those cheeks were flushed with heat, but the eyes that were glued to Russ had a shocked look in them.

"Hey, Mom," Diane called, "perfect timing. We were just having coffee. Come join us."

Russ had begun to breathe again, but

barely. Fully dressed, as she'd been last night, Cynthia had looked spectacular. She looked even more spectacular wearing so little. Her limbs were slim, well toned and lightly tanned, and if twenty-five years had added scars, liver spots or cellulite, he couldn't see any.

Aware of a quickening inside, he forced himself to inhale. The breath escaped in a shaky whoosh. "This woman can't be your mother, Diane. She's not old enough."

"She's my mom, all right, but she puts me to shame. She's so *fit* it's *disgusting.*"

"Since when has she been running?"

"Since forever. I can't remember a time when she didn't. She says it clears her head."

Russ knew that for a fact, but any benefit he had derived from his own morning run was gone. His head was filled with images of the last time he'd seen Cynthia so undressed, and his body was responding accordingly. Unable to sit down while she was standing there, yet more fearful by the minute that his arousal would be noticed, he didn't know what to do. He was relieved when Mrs. Fritz created a distraction by barreling out of the kitchen with a slam of the screen door.

Every bit as relieved as Russ, Cynthia took the towel the woman handed her and covered her face. She hadn't been prepared to find Russ there. She wasn't ready to see him again so soon. She hadn't begun to analyze the feelings that had kept her awake for a good part of the night. But because she had been awake so late, she had slept later than usual, which was why she had gone running later than usual, which was why he had caught her in such a state. Not that he wasn't seeing anything he hadn't seen before. Russ had seen her naked and sweaty — just as she had seen him aroused. But neither condition was appropriate at the moment.

After mopping at her neck and arms, she took the glass of ice water from Mrs. Fritz and drained it before handing it back. "Coffee, ma'am?" the cook asked.

"No, thanks," Cynthia murmured. She waited until the woman had gone back into the kitchen before turning to Russ. The towel hung from her hands, the only shield she had against the exposure she felt. "I'm sorry," she said softly. Her breathing may have slowed, but her body still hummed. "If I'd known you were coming, I wouldn't have barged in this way."

"It's your house," Russ said as softly. He couldn't take his eyes from her, but that was nothing new. "You can barge in whenever you want. I'm the intruder. I just wanted to stop by and say hi to Diane. And make sure you're all right."

"I'm all right."

She didn't look it. She looked as paralyzed as he felt. No, he realized, *paralyzed* was the

61

wrong word. *Mesmerized* was more like it. From day one in the soda shop, they had been captivated by each other to the extent that the rest of the world had fallen away, leaving only the two of them, drawn closer and closer. He decided now that the attraction was caused by something chemical, a magnetic response neither of them could control. He didn't imagine she wanted to be drawn to him any more than he did to her.

But Cynthia wasn't thinking about the soda shop or chemical attractions or magnetic responses just then. She had a more immediate quandary. She knew she should excuse herself and go inside, but she couldn't make herself leave. Nor could she continue to stand there. Needing more protection than the towel offered, she crossed the patio and slipped into a seat all the way across the table from Russ. With the towel draped around her neck so that its ends covered her breasts, she felt better.

Russ, too, sat. "Your house is wonderful, Cyn. Was it Matthew's before you married?"

"No. We bought it fresh. The woman who had owned it for years passed away right around the time we were looking. It needed a lot of work."

The little Russ had seen of the inside of the house was in wonderful condition, though he assumed it had been redecorated more than once since they'd bought it. "Did you have to do much with the grounds?"

"Uh-huh. Nearly everything had been neglected. Some things came back with just a little pruning. Others had to be replaced."

"Your landscape architect was brilliant."

"I didn't use a landscape architect. The ones I talked with wanted to do all kinds of lovely little things that would have given a prissy look to the place. I wanted the grounds to be lush, which, believe it or not, is easier to achieve. So I directed everything myself."

Russ was impressed, though not surprised. He had always known Cynthia could do whatever she set her mind to — and it had nothing to do with money or the confidence of the wealthy. She was a hard worker. Whether learning how to cook, keeping their tiny apartment neat and clean, caring for the baby or caring for him, what she did she did well.

"You must have designed everything with this occasion in mind," he commented. "It's a beautiful setting for a wedding. Now, if the sun cooperates —"

"It will," she said with a quick smile. "It always cooperates for weddings."

Russ's own smile was slower and filled with reflective amazement. "You were always so positive. I don't think I've ever met anyone as positive as you. When we were in school, you used to study your butt off for exams, but by the time you closed your books, you were sure you'd do well, and you always did. When we were looking for an apartment, you were sure we could find something we could afford, and we did. When we were looking for jobs, you were sure we could find ones close enough so we could meet every day for lunch, and we did." He remembered those lunches. From the affectionate look on Cynthia's face, he guessed she did, too.

"Brown paper sacks," she mused. "Peanut butter and jelly sandwiches, cream cheese and olive sandwiches or tuna sandwiches — two for you, one for me. Potato chips that were usually crushed in transit. An apple. And a thermos of chocolate milk."

"Bosco and milk," he added with a grin. "Remember that?"

She grinned back and nodded. "I always told you it would stay mixed, and it did."

"You also told me there was no rush to get to the hospital after your water broke. We were so damned laid-back that by the time we got there, you were fully dilated." He turned to Diane. "You were nearly born in the front seat —" He stopped at the sight of her eyes, which were bright with tears. "What's wrong?" he asked, instantly alarmed.

She smiled through the tears, which remained unshed. "Nothing. It's just so weird seeing you two together." Her gaze flipped to Cynthia, then back. "It kind of brings things full circle. On the eve of my wedding. That's poetic, don't you think?"

What Cynthia thought was that Diane was a gem. Some daughters might have been angry at their mothers for having made them wait so long for such an occasion. Diane merely seemed delighted that it had come, which went to prove what Cynthia had told Russ in his hotel room. Diane had never been a demanding child. Whatever she received she appreciated. She was so, so special that way.

Russ must have thought the same thing, because before Cynthia could brace herself, he hooked an elbow around Diane's neck and drew her face to his shoulder. Cynthia felt a sharp jolt inside, then a tilting sensation near her heart. This was a first for her, too — seeing father and daughter together as adults — and it affected her more deeply than she would have imagined. Russ's ease with Diane, his spontaneity, his obvious affection — he would have been a wonderful father if he had been around. She supposed the relationship was better late than never. Still, for her daughter, she felt a loss.

Marginally aware that the loss she felt was for herself, as well, she rose from her chair and started for the house.

"Cyn?"

"I have to shower," she called back. Ignoring the creak of wicker behind her, she continued on to the screen door, but before she could do more than draw it open, Russ was by her side.

"Wait." His voice was low and close. "There's something I have to ask you."

She kept her eyes on the floor, not that that helped. She didn't have to raise them to be aware of his height. It seemed he always towered over her. When they'd been eighteen, part of the towering had been in her mind. She had been in awe of him for the hardships of his upbringing and the person he was in spite of it, and she'd been in love. In theory, she was over both the awe and the love, but he was still tall. She wanted desperately to believe that it was nothing more than a physical fact.

"I'm really a mess," she told him. "I don't feel comfortable sitting out here like this."

"I've seen you looking worse."

"When we were kids. Things are different now."

"You don't have to stand on ceremony with me. I'm family."

She did raise her eyes then to meet his. "Not to me. Our marriage was annulled years ago."

Russ saw the hurt and sorrow on her face and was as surprised by their strength as he had been the night before. He would have expected her to have put the past behind her. After all, she'd gone on to marry well.

"That's . . . kind of what I wanted to ask you," he said quietly.

Her eyes widened. "About the annulment? Are you thinking of marrying again?"

"No, no. But one of the priests who'll be assisting at Diane's wedding is an old friend."

"Jackie Flynn," she breathed, then watched the corner of his mouth turn up.

"Better known on the basketball court as the Dunkin' Dubliner."

"I wouldn't try that one now, if I were you. He's Father John to his friends."

"Father John," Russ repeated in a properly subdued tone. "I wrote him that I was coming in for the wedding, and he suggested I call, which I did this morning. He's invited us to be his guests for dinner at the Ritz."

"Us?"

"That's what he said."

"*His* guests?"

"That's what he said."

"At the Ritz?"

Russ shrugged.

"That's *appalling*," she cried. "I can think of far more appropriate ways for the church to spend its money."

"That's what *I* said."

"What did he say then?"

"That we'd both made such generous contributions to the church in honor of Diane's wedding that it was the least he could do. And that the Ritz-Carlton is new in town and he wanted to eat there — and that, in fact, he wouldn't be paying a cent because he was making good on a bet he'd made with the manager."

"The rogue," Cynthia muttered, but fondly.

"That's just what I called him. So what do you say? Are you free tonight?"

"Yes, but —"

"He suggested we pick him up at the rectory at seven. Any problem?"

"No, but —"

"Good," Russ said with a sigh. "He really had his heart set on this. I wasn't looking forward to disappointing him."

"But you were the one who was his friend," Cynthia protested. She questioned the wisdom of spending any unnecessary time with Russ. Something told her that only heartache would come of it. "You'll want to talk over old times. Wouldn't it be better if the two of you went alone?"

"He said something about discussing the wedding."

"I've already discussed the wedding with him."

"He wants to discuss it with *us*."

She squeezed her eyes shut. Russ was being persistent, and she didn't know how to handle it.

"I know what you're thinking," he said in a soft, private voice, "and believe me, there's a part of me that agrees."

"That we shouldn't go?" she asked without opening her eyes.

"That we shouldn't test fate by sharing the same table." As it was, he was testing fate by leaning close enough to discover that Cynthia's scent was as sweet and alluring as ever. In an attempt to lessen the torment, he straightened and took a small step back. "But he's a priest. What better buffer could we find?"

She thought about the word *buffer* as she opened her eyes to his. *Referee* might have been a more appropriate word, if being together was going to cause the kind of heated discussion they'd had the night before. Or *chaperon,* if she didn't get used to seeing him fast. She could understand that there would be an awareness of the time of their first reunion, since sexuality had played a major role in their relationship. But that first reunion was over. This was the second. Tonight would be the third. The awareness had to die down. It *had* to.

So she thought positively. "Okay. What time should I be ready?"

"Six forty-five?"

She nodded. "I'll see you then."

Chapter Four

Cynthia spent most of the day trying to find a way to get out of dinner. But though she had deliberately left her evenings early in the wedding week free for the inevitable flurry of last-minute arrangements, there were surprisingly few. She was in daily touch with the florist and the caterer, both of whom were skilled at their jobs and perfectly calm. Tammy Farentino had been in touch with the string quartet and the band to make sure they understood exactly when and what Cynthia wanted them to play; she had also touched base with the tablecloth person, the limousine service, the photographer and the videographer. Mandy Johnson had picked up the leather-bound book that Cynthia had ordered for guests to sign on entering the church, and she'd met with the calligrapher, who was busily writing table numbers on place cards as per the seating arrangement Cynthia and Diane had finalized the weekend before. Diane was in near-daily contact with each of her attendants and had been to the bridal shop for last-minute fittings. There was a small matter of picking up the gold rosebud earrings she would be giving to each of those attendants as a gift, but that was it.

So Tuesday evening found Cynthia sitting nervously on the Louis XVI-style settee at the far end of the living room. She was wearing a simple dress of apricot-colored silk and she clutched a patterned shawl, both drawn from her closet for their dignity. After the way Russ had seen her that morning, she felt compelled to repolish her image.

The bell rang at six-forty, which didn't surprise Cynthia a bit. Russ had always been prompt to the point of being early, which was why she had been on the settee since six-thirty. She rose so quickly her heart beat double time, so she forced herself to stand still for a good ten seconds, breathing slowly in and out. When she felt she had regained a modicum of composure, she started for the door.

Robert beat her to it. He was the butler, tall and lean, with those straight lines accentuated by perfect posture and the dark gray vest and trousers he wore.

"Mrs. Bauer, please?"

Cynthia arrived at the foyer. To the butler, in a soft murmur, she said, "Thank you, Robert." He nodded to her, then to Russ, before turning and, back straight, walking toward the kitchen.

"He's a dignified-looking man," Russ remarked.

"He's Mrs. Fritz's husband."

Russ would never have paired them. "You're kidding."

"No. They've been with us for years. Robert serves not only as butler but as chauffeur, courier and handyman. He's also the keeper of the rose garden."

Russ arched a brow. "A true master of versatility." Cynthia arched a brow right back. "You could say that."

He smiled. "I'd rather say nice things about you. You look beautiful."

She said a soft thank-you, all the while reminding herself that compliments were a dime a dozen, that Russ's was nothing special and that the rapid thump-thump of her heart was left over from the anticipation that had built while she'd waited for him to arrive. Without quite planning it, though, she heard herself say, "You look terrific yourself." Her expression grew bemused as she took in his navy summer suit, crisp white shirt and paisley tie.

"What?"

"You look so —" she raised her eyes to his face "— so grown-up."

He grinned. "I am grown-up."

"I know, but the picture I carried in my mind all these years was of you at eighteen. To suddenly see you at forty-three is strange."

She gave a tiny frown, but it held the same

bemusement of moments before. "I don't think I've ever seen you in a suit."

"I'd never owned one when we were together."

"It looks . . ." she struggled to find the right word, only to go with the simple and eloquent ". . . great."

His grin grew lopsided. "Thanks." He actually looked slightly embarrassed, but endearingly so. He had never been at all cocky. She remembered the way he used to blush when she said personal, intimate things, and the way she had loved it when he did. Though he wasn't quite blushing now, she loved the expression on his face nonetheless, particularly in light of the very sophisticated way the rest of him looked. She felt she had connected once again with the boy he had been — which was only right, since part of her felt like the girl she had been, young and starry-eyed and excited by the thought of being with Russ. Memory. That was all it was, she told herself. Forcing her eyes from his, she glanced at the slim gold watch on her wrist. "Would you like a drink before we leave?"

"No, thanks. I have a feeling John will be offering us something at the rectory. Our reservations aren't until eight. Are you all set to go?"

Taking a small evening bag from the antique table by the door, she nodded. Moments later she was tucked into Russ's car and they were on their way.

The rectory was a modest stone house behind the church. John Flynn was waiting for them, but the look on his face wasn't as easygoing as Cynthia had come to expect from the man. He did produce a smile and a warm handclasp for her, and when he turned to Russ, there was mischief in his eyes and genuine affection in the bear hug he gave.

"Gee, Russ, it's good to see you!" he said, then repeated the words with several hearty shoulder slaps. But his smile faded soon afterward, and his gaze moved from Russ's face to Cynthia and back. "I was so looking forward to tonight, but it appears the Ritz will have to wait — for me, at least. I received a call twenty minutes ago from one of my parishioners. There's been a serious accident."

"Oh, dear," Cynthia said, wondering which of his parishioners it was and whether she knew the person. She knew many of the people who lived in the area. Father John was aware of that. She guessed that if he wanted her to know who'd been hurt, he would tell her. "An automobile accident?"

"No, it was a construction accident. A fluky thing, from the little I was told, but my source was quite upset. I promised I would be at the hospital as soon as possible. I tried calling the house to save you the trip here, but you had already left, and I didn't want to be on my way without speaking with you myself." He looked at Russ. "I'm sorry. I feel terrible standing you up."

Russ knew what it was to have emergencies. "Don't apologize, John. More than once in the past year I've been called from an evening engagement to see to an emergency at one of the dorms. Certain jobs demand that you be on call. Yours is one of those jobs. I'm only sorry we'll miss this chance to talk."

"We'll have to reschedule, that's all," John said. "And in the meanwhile, you two will go on to the Ritz tonight as my guests."

Cynthia came to attention. "Oh, no, Father John, we couldn't possibly do that."

"But it's all arranged," he insisted. "The manager owes me. I've already talked with him. He's expecting you."

Russ was feeling as uncomfortable as Cynthia. "Why don't we just rereserve. Are you free tomorrow night?"

The priest shook his head. "Not tomorrow or Thursday night, either, since I believe we all have a wedding rehearsal, then dinner at Granatelli's Restaurant." To Cynthia he said, "And you're not going to want to go out the night before the wedding."

"I don't dare," she said apologetically. "Annie D'Angelo will be at the house, along with who knows how many more of the bridesmaids. Diane may be nervous. I feel I should be available in case she needs me."

"So you'll go to the Ritz tonight," John instructed, "and you'll report back to me on how it is." He turned to Russ. "Can we talk at the rehearsal dinner?"

"Sure thing."

"I still don't think we should go without you," Cynthia said. The thought of being alone with Russ was making her stomach jump. "What good is a bet if you can't collect on it."

"I'm collecting," John told her.

"But for *you*."

"I'm a priest. Given the vows I took, the Ritz is a little too much, don't you think? Besides," he added with a mischievous gleam, "that bet had to do with the Blues. I've got another one going on the Cardinals that's a sure winner, too." He put an arm around each of them and, becoming more serious, turned them back toward the car. "My evening is apt to be difficult. It'll give me great pleasure thinking of you at dinner. Would you deny me that pleasure?"

"That's blackmail," Cynthia chided, but fondly.

As fondly, Russ added, "I can see that the old Jackie Flynn is alive and well behind that Roman collar of yours."

With an unrepentant grin, John dropped his arms to open the car door for Cynthia. "The good Lord understands that even the most pious of men aren't saints."

Cynthia slid into the passenger seat. "What

fun will it be for us without you?"

John shut the door and leaned down to the open window. "You'll make your fun. I seem to recall a time when you guys didn't want *anyone* around."

"Those days are long gone," she said with a wisp of sadness, then, before he could add anything, covered his hand with hers. "We'll be thinking of you tonight. I hope everything turns out well."

"So do I," he said, and looked at Russ. "Thursday night?"

"You got it." Russ started the car and drove off. He hadn't gone more than a block when he realized what the Dunkin' Dubliner had done and what it meant. He'd passed Russ the ball and was expecting him to take it down the court. But damn, it was a long time since Russ had played the game, and the stakes were *so high.*

Silence reigned for another block, by which time he was desperate to know what Cynthia was thinking. So he said, "That's too bad. I was looking forward to talking with John. I wonder who's been hurt."

Cynthia's thoughts had been on the so-grown-up man by her side and the evening ahead. At Russ's reminder, she felt instant guilt. Some poor soul was struggling for his life while she was debating the pros and cons of showing up at St. Louis's new Ritz-Carlton on the arm of her onetime husband.

Turning her gaze to the window and away from Russ's too-imposing presence, she shrugged. "A fluky accident, he said. That's scary. I always used to worry that something fluky would happen to Diane." She reconsidered the words. "I used to worry that something *not fluky* would happen to her, too." Reconsidering yet again, she finally admitted, "I used to worry, period. There are times when I still do. She may be twenty-five and off on her own, but if I let myself think about her in New York City, I go a little nuts. I'm glad she'll have Nick with her from now on."

"Don't tell her that. She'll say she's perfectly capable of taking care of herself."

"Still, I worry. Not all the time. Only when I think."

Russ was about to say that was a mother's prerogative, when he shot her a glance. She was diligently keeping her head angled toward the window, but her profile was lovely enough to drive the words from his mind. Long after he returned his eyes to the road, he saw that profile, and felt increasingly confused. He was looking forward to the evening. He was looking forward to it too much.

"Cyn, if you'd rather not go to dinner . . . I mean, if being with me is going to make you uncomfortable, I can take you back home."

She lowered her eyes. Uncomfortable? Was

that what she was feeling? She didn't think so. She didn't think it was possible for her to feel uncomfortable with Russ for long. He was too easy to be with, too accommodating, too interesting. When they'd been seniors in high school, she had wanted to know all about his life and his classes and his extracurricular activities. Twenty-five years later, she wanted to know the very same things.

There was danger, of course. He still turned her on. She could feel the pull even though — it stunned her to realize — he hadn't touched her once, not once, since that last night twenty-five years before when they'd made love. They hadn't shaken hands last night at his hotel. He hadn't so much as touched her arm to stop her from leaving the patio that morning or, when he'd picked her up tonight, laid a hand on her waist to guide her to the car.

"Cyn?"

The pull was still there. His voice touched all the places his hands hadn't, and his eyes touched more. But she could handle it. She was *determined* to handle it. With all that had been going on in preparation for the wedding, she deserved a quiet, private dinner, and who more appropriate to have that quiet, private dinner with than the father of the bride? Besides, she was curious. She had gotten glimpses of what Russ had done with his life. She wanted to hear more.

"I can handle it," she sighed, more to herself than to him.

The sigh hit him the wrong way. "Don't do me any favors," he muttered.

She shot him a surprised look. "Why do you say that?"

"Because I'm not so hard up for company that I can't eat alone."

"I said I'd come."

His eyes clung to the road and his hands to the wheel. "But you sound like it's the last thing you want, and if that's so, I'd *rather* eat alone."

"Maybe you'd rather eat alone, anyway. You sound like you're looking for an out."

"I'm not. I think you are."

She faced him more fully. "Why would I want an out?"

"Because you're uncomfortable with me."

"Did I say I was?"

"No, but you wouldn't. You're trained not to say things like that."

"Where you're concerned I'll say anything I want!"

He scowled. "Right, and maybe that's why we shouldn't go to dinner together. You're angry at me for something that happened twenty-five years ago. You couldn't keep it in last night, and you probably won't be able to tonight."

"Because it still hurts!"

"Twenty-five years later?"

"Yes!"

"You should be over it."

"I thought I was, but seeing you brings it back."

"It shouldn't, damn it," he said, feeling angry. "Twenty-five years is too long a time for something like that to linger."

"Twenty-five years is *nothing* when people feel things like we did! Do you mean to tell me you didn't feel a thing after the night you left? That you didn't ever think of us over the years and feel a sense of loss? That you didn't ever wake up in the middle of the night with a longing so intense that you'd have turned a cold shower hot?" As soon as the words were out, Cynthia was appalled. But it was too late to take them back, and she wasn't sure she would have, anyway. She was being honest. No one could condemn her for that. "If you can truly say that you got over us —" she snapped her fingers "— like that, something was wrong, very wrong with the way we were then. Was it all a sham?"

Her words echoed in the car for the longest time before Russ could react. When he did, it was with carefully controlled movements, pulling the vehicle to the side of the road, letting the engine idle. He dropped his hands to his lap and stared at the center of the steering wheel. An air bag was packed there. In case of an accident, it would inflate and save his life — and he would want it to. But that hadn't always been so.

"It wasn't a sham," he said quietly. "What we had was the most beautiful thing I've ever known. There were times when the loss I felt was nearly unbearable. There were times during the war when I honestly didn't give a damn whether I made it home or not. Someone was watching out for me there, because I sure as hell wasn't. When I got back in one piece, I decided I owed that Someone for what He had done. So I worked harder in school, and after that at work, than I might have done otherwise. I had no one to do it for. You were lost to me — by my own hand — and if you think you were the only one lying awake at night, you're dead wrong. There were nights I wanted you so bad I swear I almost flew back here."

His lower lip came out to cover the upper one. Slowly it slipped down again. "You're right. Twenty-five years isn't long at all with feelings that strong. When I suggested it was, I was trying to deny things I've been feeling myself since I saw you last night." He hesitated, unsure of how much to say. But one of the most beautiful things about his relationship with Cynthia had been its openness. They had poured out their hearts and souls to each other. There was nothing they hadn't shared — except his decision to leave. In terms of forthrightness, he owed her one. So he confessed, "Everything's come back. I didn't plan on it happening. I didn't want it to. But it's there."

Cynthia sat much as he did, with her hands in her lap and her eyes straight ahead. She wanted to look at him but didn't dare. His words alone had a powerful effect on her. "Maybe it's memory. Maybe what we're feeling now is just the memory of what we felt then."

"Maybe."

"Maybe it's just a residual from things that went unresolved after you left."

"Maybe."

"Maybe it's not what we really feel — I mean, what you and I feel as the individuals we are today. Maybe it's all for old times' sake."

"Maybe." He raised his eyes to the windshield. "So how do we handle it?"

"I don't know." Still staring straight ahead, she threw the question back at him. "You were always the sensible one. How do we handle it?"

He thought hard, trying to separate what his mind recommended from what his heart did, only to realize there wasn't much difference between the two. "I think we have to talk. We have to get to know each other as we are now. We have to put reality between us and the past. Could be that once we get to know each other, we'll find a comfortable middle ground to stand on."

"Somewhere between attraction and antagonism?"

"Right."

"Do you think that's possible?"

"Yes. We're neither of us antagonistic people."

"About the other," she said in a smaller voice, because she could still feel it, could still feel the pull.

Russ didn't have to ask what she meant. He could feel it, too. Slowly he turned his head, and the sight of her heightened the feeling. He had dreamed about her over the years, and come morning had always pushed her image from his mind. But she was here. With him. After all those years of dreams.

"I think it still exists," he said in a voice so low she might not have heard if there had been any noise outside the car. But it was a lazy June evening. Traffic was light. The only noise was the whisper of cool air coming from the vents, and that coolness wasn't nearly enough to take the edge off his heat. "Look at me, Cyn."

After a moment's reluctance, she turned her head. What she saw in his eyes reflected what she was feeling inside, and it nearly broke her apart. She held her breath when he raised his hand. It hovered for a minute before ever so lightly touching her cheek, then curving around her neck. His thumb brushed her mouth.

"It still exists," he said, hoarsely this time.

"I know," she whispered.

"But we're adults now. We can resist it."

"We have to. I don't think I can bear the pain again."

"But what about the glory?" He was thinking about the way she had always taken him out of himself and elevated him to a plane where everything was breathtakingly beautiful. "Wouldn't you like a taste of that again?"

"Oh, God." She was being drawn in by his smoky eyes, his sandy voice, the spray of silver in his hair — and the silver hadn't been there before, which shot the theory of memory turning them on. She wanted him to kiss her, wanted it more than anything in the world at that moment.

It was her turn to raise a hand, then hesitate. Then she put her fingertips on his lips, moved them over his cheek to his temple, then back by his ear.

He drew in a shuddering breath and trapped her hand on his neck. "Don't tempt me, Cyn. Don't tell me it's okay. I haven't changed much where you're concerned. I never could resist when you touched me. Given the choice, I'd take you back to my hotel room right now and to hell with dinner. But I don't think that's wise."

One part of Cynthia wondered. That part would opt for the hotel room, too, on the premise that what was building between them simply had to be released to be gone. The other part was worried it wouldn't ever be gone, and she didn't know what she'd do then.

Retrieving her hand and anchoring it on her lap, she said, "You're right. Let's go to dinner." The words were rushed, she knew. Russ had to know she was torn. But he didn't say anything more. She was infinitely grateful when he put the car in gear and moved off.

"Tell me about your life," Russ said. Having arrived at the Ritz in advance of their reservations, they were having drinks at the bar.

Cynthia took a slow sip of her martini. She felt much safer now that they were out of the confines of the car and surrounded by other people. "That's a tall order. Where should I start?"

"At the beginning." He wanted to know all the things the newspaper hadn't covered. "When I left."

She ran her thumb along the rim of the glass. "At the time I thought that was the end, not the beginning. I was so happy with you, then you were gone. I was sure life would go totally downhill from there."

Russ knew there would be pain in what she had to say, but he needed to know. What had happened after he left was all part of who she was now. "What did your mother say when you showed up at her door?"

"I called first. I didn't have the courage to show up without knowing whether she would let me in. If she rejected me after you had —"

"I didn't reject you."

"That's what it felt like to me at the time," Cynthia argued, then purposefully gentled her voice. She didn't want to be angry at Russ. All she wanted was to make him understand. "I was feeling very vulnerable. So I called her." She stopped then, remembering back to that sticky July day and the phone booth that had looked so dirty next to Diane's baby-soft skin.

"What did you say to her?" Russ asked quietly.

She sighed. "Actually nothing. I started to cry. She got the message. I managed to tell her where I was. She was there in ten minutes."

"You should have called her sooner."

Cynthia shook her head. "I couldn't. It took that month alone before I could face her."

Russ took a swallow of Scotch and jiggled the ice in his glass for a minute before he said, "I wanted you to go home, because I

87

knew she would take care of you, but I was worried that she would make things impossible for you in the process."

"Like drilling my stupidity into me?"

"Yeah."

"She didn't. She didn't say a word about that. She really did play her cards perfectly. I was heartbroken that you'd left, and she could see that. She made things so easy for me at home that when I finally came out of my blue funk, I was ready to be the kind of daughter she wanted."

Russ wondered who had taken care of Diane while Cynthia had been in her "blue funk." She had been totally devoted to the baby when he'd been around. "I suppose you weaned Diane to a bottle pretty quickly, huh?"

"I nursed her until her first birthday."

He was inordinately pleased by that fact. As an afterthought, he grinned. "What did Gertrude think of that?"

Cynthia's mouth twitched. "What do you think she thought?"

"That it was a vulgar practice fitting only for peasants."

"That's pretty much it." Her eyes grew serious. "But what she thought didn't matter when it came to Diane. Diane was mine. I took care of her. She was the only peace of mind I had in those days."

The pain was there again. Russ wondered

if they'd ever be able to escape it. "When did you meet Matthew?"

"When I was little, long before I met you. He was sixteen years older than me, but he moved in the same circles as my family. I was with Diane at the club one day — she was eighteen months old — and he and I started to talk. We were engaged two months later and married seven months after that."

"Why the seven-month wait? Was it so that Diane could get used to him?"

Cynthia shook her head. "They took to each other right from the start." She turned her glass on its cocktail napkin. "My mother wanted to do everything she had been denied the first time. There were engagement parties and postengagement parties and showers and prewedding dinners. She was in her glory."

"Were you?" he asked. He knew it was a loaded question, but the answer mattered.

She raised her eyes to his. "Was I in my glory? No. Did I enjoy myself? Yes. I never rejected my world when I married you. That world, thanks to my mother, rejected me. But I'd been raised with those people. I fitted back in. There were — are — many of them I really like. Sure, I had to deal with some shallow people, but there are shallow people at every level. I surrounded myself with the ones who weren't. They're the ones who work with me on fund-raisers for the art museum and the cancer society. They're the ones who helped me raise money for the homeless long before it became fashionable to do so." She gave a slow, sure shake of her head. "I make no apologies for what I did then or at any time since."

For a minute Russ couldn't think of a thing to say. He wanted to criticize her for taking the pleasure she had. After all, while she had been lifting canapés from silver trays, he had been slogging through rice paddies. But she was eloquent in her defense of the life she had lived. If she had made the best of the circumstances, using her position in society to benefit worthy causes, he couldn't find fault. He had to respect her for acting on her beliefs.

"Excuse me? Dr. Shaw?"

Russ swung his head around, and he found himself confronting a familiar-looking man. In a matter of seconds he placed him — the father of one of his students. With a smile, he rose from the bar stool and extended his hand. "It's odd seeing people out of context. I've only seen you in Connecticut, my own neck of the woods. But Chris is very definitely from St. Louis. How are you, Mr. Mason?"

"Very well, thanks, and the feeling's mutual. I've been sitting over there with my friends watching you, wondering if you were who I thought. I didn't expect to see you so far from home."

"I'm here for a wedding," Russ said. "Do you know Cynthia Bauer? Cyn, this is Phillip Mason. He's the father of one of my more promising sophomores."

Cynthia smiled and let the man take her hand. "We've been introduced before, I believe." She frowned, trying to remember exactly when and where. "Don't you sit with the Grahams at Powell Hall?"

"You have a good memory," Mason commented. "Powell Hall it was. And aren't you the one putting on the wedding?"

"That's right."

Releasing her hand, he pointed a thumb at Russ. "So what's his connection?"

With a serenity that stunned Russ, she said, "He's the father of the bride."

It wasn't a secret exactly. But someone like Phillip Mason, who had known Cynthia only as Mrs. Matthew Bauer and Diane as Diane Bauer, wouldn't necessarily know the truth. Indeed, the look on his face was priceless. His eyes lighted in surprise one minute, then grew perplexed the next, and when he opened his mouth to say something polite, nothing came out.

Russ, who was counting on the man to give a significant contribution to his school's Annual Fund that year, took pity on him. "Cynthia was my child bride. Diane was born shortly before we separated."

"I hadn't realized," Mason murmured. To

Cynthia, he added, "I simply assumed Diane was Matthew's."

"Most people do," she said kindly.

Russ was reassured by her tone. So, apparently, was Phillip Mason, because he grew confident again. "She is one lucky young lady to have this man as her father. For years he's been one of Hollings's best teachers, and now he's proving to be a top-notch headmaster. You can tell her I said that." He turned to Russ. "Will you be in town long?"

"Only until Sunday."

"If you're free, we'd love to have you out at the house."

"That might be difficult. It's a short trip with a lot to do, but thanks for offering. Has Chris left for the Southwest yet?" He had been trying to remember what the younger Mason was doing for the summer. With more than three hundred students enrolled at the school, it was hard to know about each, but Russ did recall something about an archeological dig in Arizona.

"Next Tuesday. He's looking forward to it."

"Will you give him my best and wish him a wonderful trip for me?"

"I certainly will." Mason slapped him on the back. "You have a good summer, and congratulations to you both —" he broadened his gaze to include Cynthia "— on your daughter's wedding."

"Thank you," Cynthia said. As the man

walked away, she couldn't help but consider the irony of being in one of St. Louis's newest and poshest hotels with Russell Shaw and having *him* be the one recognized. Not that it bothered her. To the contrary. She felt a glimmer of pride. Apparently he had made quite something of his life. She wanted to know more.

"Tell me about *your* life," she said. They were seated at a pleasantly private table, but the privacy wasn't bothering Cynthia. They had already been visited by the manager, the maître d', the wine steward, the waiter and the busboy. She was grateful for the momentary respite, during which she was hoping to learn something about the father of her daughter.

"That's a tall order," he drawled, echoing her earlier words. "Where should I start?"

"With your discharge from the army."

"What do you already know?" He wasn't the arrogant type. The last thing he wanted to do was to repeat old information.

"Only that you're Dr. Shaw and that you're headmaster at the Hollings Academy in Connecticut."

He would have thought she'd know more. Diane certainly did. He felt vaguely hurt that she hadn't been curious over the years. God knew he had been about her. "In a nutshell, I got my B.A. from Georgetown and went to teach history at Hollings. Over the years, I picked up an M.A., then a Ph.D. I was named headmaster last year."

She didn't seem at all daunted by his curtness. Her eyes were wide and expectant. "Go on."

"With what?"

"Why you chose teaching, why history, why Hollings, how you came to be headmaster, whether you like the job."

"I can't answer those in order."

"Why not?"

"Because they sound like they'd be a chronological succession, but they're not. I chose history because it fascinates me."

"It always did," she said, remembering. "You were good at it."

"Because it fascinated me. So I was getting ready to graduate with a degree in it, and the most obvious thing to do was to teach, but I was feeling unsettled. Homeless. Insecure. I had gone straight from the army to Georgetown, and for the first time in six years I didn't know where I was going. Then I heard about the opening at Hollings and went to visit the place. That was it. I was sold."

"What's it like?"

His mood softened as he thought of the school. "Green, very green. And warm. It's like a college campus in miniature, with tree-lined walks connecting one old stone building to the next. There's a feeling of history to it. And a sense of caring. When I first went there, it was all boys. More than half of them board, which means the school has to take the place of parents and family. And it does. More than anything, I think that was what appealed to me — the caring, the camaraderie between students and students, students and faculty. Hollings gave me a family. It also gave me a place to stay."

"You had an apartment on campus?"

"It was a two-room job in one of the dorms. It was furnished, so I didn't have to buy anything, and I got extra money by being a dorm parent."

"Was it hard work?"

"Not if you like kids, and I like kids."

"I never knew that," Cynthia said with a bemused look.

"Neither did I while I knew you. We were kids ourselves."

"When did you find out?"

"When I was at Georgetown. I took part in a volunteer project with inner-city kids. Those kids were tough, but they were great. Obviously the kids at Hollings were different, but they were great, too."

"So you stayed on. Did you take time off when you did your degree work?"

He shook his head. "I did it evenings and summers."

"That must have been hard."

He shrugged. "I didn't have anything else to do with my free time."

"Didn't you date?" she asked. He was such a strikingly handsome man. She couldn't believe that single women would come within range of him and not look twice.

"Some."

"Were there many female teachers?"

"Some. More now, since we've gone coed."

"When did that happen?"

Russ told her, then, when another question came, answered that, too. With the natural flow of her curiosity, he found himself relaxing. Their waiter brought rolls, then salads, and through it Cynthia was enrapt with piecing together a picture of his life. More than once, basking in her enthusiasm, he was taken back to their days together. Enthusiasm had been a mainstay of her personality then. He was relieved that that hadn't changed.

They were interrupted again, twice actually, when acquaintances of Cynthia's approached their table. Though Russ would have been happier without the intrusions, Cynthia was so apologetic each time that he couldn't be angry. Besides, she always picked up where they'd left off, letting him know that her interest was real, and in that, making him feel ten feet tall.

That was pretty much the way he ended the evening. By the time he returned Cynthia to her elegant, ivy-covered house, he felt just as high as he had after spending an hour with her at the soda shop — and as horny. Sitting across from her at an intimate table for two for the better part of three hours, watching the graceful shift of her hands, the gentle movement of her mouth, the curves of her shoulders and breasts, had taken its toll. His blood was hot and racing.

Cynthia was suffering a similar fate. As Russ walked her to her door, her heart was beating far faster than she wanted. After stepping inside, she turned back, hesitantly, to look up at him. "Thank you, Russ," she said softly. "It's been a really nice evening."

"I thought so, too." He wanted to kiss her but didn't dare. One kiss wouldn't be enough. It would never be enough when the lips involved were Cynthia's and his. But neither of them was ready for more. Too much shaky ground remained between them. Still, he couldn't bear the thought of waiting two days, until the wedding rehearsal on Thursday, to see her. It would be a waste of precious time. "I'm having breakfast with Diane and Nick tomorrow. Join us?"

Cynthia would have liked that if she trusted herself, but she didn't where Russ was concerned. She was feeling overwhelmed by things she hadn't felt in years. She needed time to think.

Doing her best not to drown in his gaze,

she said, "I'd better not. I have an early meeting with Tammy, and besides, you haven't had much time with them. I don't want to take away from that."

"You wouldn't be taking away. You'd be adding."

"I'd better not."

"I'd really like it if you came."

But she shook her head. She had to be firm, had to act with her mind rather than her heart. She couldn't afford to be hurt the way she'd been hurt before. A second time she might not recover.

Chapter Five

Russ knew all about acting from the mind rather than the heart. Over the years he had given lectures aplenty on the subject to his students and knew all the words to use. He had acted with his mind on the night he'd walked away from Cynthia — and when he'd joined the army, when he'd enrolled at Georgetown, when he'd taken a job at Hollings. Acting with one's mind meant considering every angle of a situation and making the most sensible decision. It meant acting deliberately rather than on impulse.

He thought he had done that when he refrained from kissing Cynthia good-night at her door. They weren't ready for a deeper involvement. The potential for warped judgment was too great. They were seeing each other for the first time in twenty-five years, a highly charged situation on its own. Add to that the emotion of their daughter's wedding and the highly charged situation increased in voltage. They were prime candidates for making a mistake.

So his mind said.

His heart said that it wouldn't be making a

mistake at all but correcting one made long before.

His body pretty much echoed that conviction, with reverberations that lingered through the night and into the morning. When he arrived at the house to pick up Diane, he looked out for Cynthia, but she was nowhere in sight. She had a meeting with Tammy, she'd said. So he looked for her again when he brought Diane back after a thoroughly enjoyable breakfast with Nick.

"Think your mother's home yet?" he asked in a nonchalant way when he didn't see her wandering about.

"I doubt it," Diane said. "She had a list of things to do." She grew cautious. "Is everything all right?"

"Fine. I was going to offer to help, that's all."

"Aren't you spending the day with your professor friend?"

He nodded. "But I'll be free by four. I'm feeling a little fraudulent, accepting the title of father of the bride without doing any of the work. Haven't you got anything for me to do?"

"You're a guest. You don't have to work."

"I'm the father of the bride, and I *want* to work."

"Most everything's arranged for. Mom is good at that."

"Efficient."

"Very."

Frustrated by the fact, he frowned. "It's a bad habit to get into, Diane. Take my advice. When it comes to Nick, be helpless sometimes. Men like that."

She gave him a lopsided grin. "Modern women aren't helpless. For that matter, traditional women aren't helpless, either. They just pretend to be for the sake of their men. Nick isn't like that. He loves my independence."

"He loves everything about you," Russ corrected. Seeing them together over breakfast had reinforced his first impression of Nick. His daughter would be in kind, caring, capable hands — and he didn't give a damn about Diane's talk of independence. A man needed to be needed.

That thought stuck in his mind throughout the day, dallying there along with thoughts of Cynthia. He met with Evan Waldman, who had taught at Hollings before moving to St. Louis, but no matter how engrossing their talk, at the slightest break in the conversation Russ's mind wandered. On his drive back to the hotel later that day, he actually took a detour past Cynthia's. But he didn't stop. He hadn't been invited, didn't think he was needed, refused to make a fool of himself.

It was a matter of mind versus heart again. He stuck with his mind's decision through a dinner he barely ate, until loneliness eroded his resolve. This time, when he drove to

Cynthia's, he pulled right up to the door and parked.

Robert answered with a genteel, "Good evening, sir."

"How are you tonight, Robert?"

"Just fine, thank you, sir."

"Is Mrs. Bauer in?"

"I believe so. If you'll come in and have a seat —" he showed him into the living room "— I'll let her know you're here."

"Thank you." Russ lowered himself to the settee but sat on its edge, his elbows on his knees. He shouldn't have come. She was going to be annoyed.

As it happened, Cynthia wasn't at all annoyed. To the contrary. If she had been able to wish for one thing, it would have been to see him just then. With a tired smile she leaned against the living room arch. "Hi."

He got quickly to his feet. "Hi." His eyes scanned her face. "What's wrong?"

She scrunched up her nose and took a deep breath. "Ooooh, it's been a bit of a rough day."

"Last-minute glitches?"

"In a way." She wrapped her arms around her waist. "You know the accident Father John mentioned last night?"

Russ nodded.

"The boy who was injured is the son of one of my friends."

He came closer. "I'm sorry, Cyn. I didn't

know. Diane didn't say anything this morning."

"She didn't know. *We* didn't know. They kept things quiet until midday."

Tucking his hands in the pockets of his slacks, he came closer still. "What happened?"

"The boy's father — my friend's husband — is a developer. He got Jimmy a summer job working at one of his building sites. Scaffolding collapsed. Jimmy fell."

"How badly hurt is he?"

"They still don't know for sure. He's in a coma." Her eyes teared. "He's twenty years old with a whole life ahead of him if only he wakes up . . . and they were worrying about telling me, because they didn't want to put a damper on Diane's wedding week." She pressed a hand to her upper lip, which had begun to tremble.

Thinking only that he'd finally found a way to help, Russ reached out and drew her to him. "Good friends do things like that."

Against his shirt, she murmured, "I've been at the hospital for most of the afternoon. There isn't anything they can do but wait. They're positively distraught."

Russ knew that Cynthia was, too. He rubbed her back, willing her to relax against him. When she did, he rewarded her with a kiss by her ear. "I'm sure it meant a lot to them that you were there."

"I wouldn't have been anywhere else." She moaned. "They kept talking about having to miss the wedding and mess up the seating arrangement. Can you believe that? For God's sake. I'd redo the arrangement ten times over if it would make Jimmy better."

"I'm sure you would," he said, and continued to hold her. She felt so right in his arms. She always had, but now even more so. He had missed the way she nestled against him. He hadn't realized how much. Through a tight throat, he whispered, "Want to take a walk?"

She didn't lift her head. "Now?"

"Yes, now."

"It'll be getting dark soon."

"We still have an hour. Better still, how about a run?"

"A run?"

"Have you had one today?"

"Early this morning." She sighed. "Feels like an aeon ago."

"Then put on your gear, we'll go back to my hotel while I change, and I'll show you the route I've been taking."

She drew her head back. "You've been taking?"

"I run, too." He gave her a little nudge and stepped back. "Go on. It'll make you feel better."

What made Cynthia feel better was the realization that, on top of everything else that drew them together, they had this in common. She did feel like running, but she wouldn't have done it alone so late. Russ's company was a gift.

Less than thirty minutes later, they were running side by side. He tempered his pace to one he felt would be comfortable for her, then picked up a little when he saw that she could handle more. When he felt they'd hit stride, he asked, "How're you doin'?"

"Great," she said, breathing easily. "Feels good."

"It always does."

"Especially when you're down. That call shook me today."

"I could see that."

She ran on a bit before saying, "Life is so fragile. Things can be fine one day and shattered the next."

"Was that how it was with Matthew?"

"Uh-huh." Matthew's heart had been the culprit. It had ticked fine on Monday and stopped cold on Tuesday. "We weren't prepared."

"Is anyone ever prepared for death?" Russ gestured for her to turn right at the corner. "You had a good life with Matthew."

"He was a kind man."

"I'm surprised you didn't have more kids."

She was a minute in answering. "Me, too. I was so quick to get pregnant with Diane. I guess I wasn't meant to have more."

"Did you want more?"

"Uh-huh." But even as the word came out, she felt hesitant. Though she had never used birth control with Matthew, neither of them had been disturbed when she hadn't conceived. "With his being older, it was probably for the best."

"You could have more now."

Between strides, she shot him a doubtful look. "I'm forty-three."

"Easily done in this day and age."

She shot him another look, a chiding one this time. "Spoken like a man." Which he was. Quite definitely. She didn't have to shoot him another look to see the dark rumple of his hair, the lean strength of his shoulders, the muscular tone of his legs. "How about you? Didn't you want other children?"

"I've had hundreds over the years."

"Of your own."

He mulled over the question. "I wasn't sure I was worthy."

"Are you kidding?" She tried to make out his expression, but dusk shadowed his face.

His voice was sober, punctuated only by the rhythm of his pace. "I abandoned Diane. I wasn't sure I deserved another child. It's taken six years of building a relationship with her to give me back a little self-respect in that regard."

"So you want more kids now?"

He shrugged, shot a look behind him for traffic and gestured for her to make a left turn. "Got no wife."

"Which mystifies me. You should have married again."

"Didn't want to. No one would be good enough. You're a hard act to follow."

Her voice went breathless. "Don't say that."

"It's the truth."

"I have my faults."

"Like what?"

"Cowardice."

"When?"

"When you left." She didn't speak for several beats. "I should have stood up to my mother."

"You weren't in a position to do that. You said it yourself."

"I know. Still, I should have. Somehow."

As confessions went, it was filled with regret and, in that, was a world away from the anger he'd heard two nights before. Gone, too, was the bitterness he'd always felt when, in moments of self-pity, he allowed himself to think she could have done something to bring him back. They were moving on, past the pain, as they needed to do if they hoped to know each other in the here and now.

One shadow of the past, though, hadn't budged. "Cyn?"

"Hmm?"

"Does your mother know I'm here?"

"Not yet."

"But she knows I'm coming to the wedding."

"Yes."

"Does she know I'm walking Diane down the aisle?"

Cynthia ran on in silence.

"She doesn't," he said.

"See what a coward I am?"

He rallied to her defense. "You didn't know about it yourself until Monday."

"I should have called her then." The syncopated pat of their running shoes on the pavement was the only sound until she tacked on, "Then again, maybe it's best she not know. She can't make much of a fuss with everyone watching at the wedding." After another minute she darted Russ an uneasy look. "Can she?"

Russ didn't know, but the more he thought about it — which he did at some length after dropping Cynthia back home that night — the more he realized he didn't want to leave the matter to chance. Gertrude Hoffmann could be one unpleasant lady. Her narrow-mindedness had sabotaged his marriage. He wasn't letting it mar his daughter's wedding day.

To that end, he showed up at her house early the next morning. He remembered the way, having dropped Cynthia back there dozens of times. More often than not he had parked down the street and walked her to the house, so that Gertrude wouldn't hear the distinctly lower-class rumble of his car. Only once had he been inside.

He remembered being impressed by the size, the shine and the sophistication. But he'd been a boy then, and raw. Now he was a man with polish of his own, and while he could appreciate the stateliness of Gertrude Hoffmann's home, he wasn't terribly impressed. Cynthia's, which held an inherent warmth, was far more to his liking.

"My name is Russell Shaw," he told the uniformed maid who answered the door. "Mrs. Hoffmann isn't expecting me, but I'd like a word with her if she's home."

He was shown into the parlor, which amused him no end. The maid didn't know who he was, but making a judgment based on his clothing, his carriage and his confidence, had deemed him safe to let in. That was a switch from the judgment made twenty-six years before.

After no more than a minute, she returned. "If you'll come this way, Mr. Shaw." She led him across the hall and down a corridor into the dining room. There, at the far end of a huge table, at a place set with fine linen, bone china and sterling silver, sat Gertrude Hoffmann — and for a split second Russ understood what Diane had said about the woman being alone. There was no sadder image than that of a solitary figure amid opulence.

Then the second passed, and he saw a woman in her mid-sixties, well preserved and imperious-looking still. Her hair was pure white and perfectly coiffed, her face neatly made up, her blue blouse impeccably starched. She was in the middle of a breakfast of eggs and toast that had come from a scrolled chafing dish nearby. But her fork had been placed neatly across her plate and she was sitting back in her chair, elbows on its arms, fingers laced, staring at him.

"I was wondering whether you'd make it over here," she announced boldly. "If I were a gambling woman, I'd have lost money. I didn't think you'd have the courage to face me after all these years."

Russ wasn't put off by her bluntness. It dispensed with polite greetings and told him just where he stood. "I have the courage. I've always had it."

"Even when you deserted my daughter and granddaughter?" she asked archly.

With confidence, he said, "Mostly then. Leaving Cynthia and Diane was the hardest thing I've ever had to do. They were all I cared about in the world. More than anything I wanted to stay with them, but that would have been the selfish thing — the cowardly thing to do. I couldn't give them what they needed or deserved, or what I wanted them to have. Not without your help. So I sent them back to you. The way I see it, that took courage. The way I see it, you should be thanking me."

Her chin lifted a notch. "For embarrassing me? For causing upheaval in my home?"

"For returning your daughter to you, and for giving you a granddaughter who is better than either of us. She's the reason I'm here today. I love Diane. This is a special time for her. If there is to be unpleasantness, I want it to stay between you and me. She isn't to feel it."

Gertrude's gaze didn't waver, though her chin dropped slightly. "She was very angry with me for a while, all because of you."

"Justly so. You had no business telling her that I was dead. She had a right to know the truth."

"To what end? So she could chase after a man who had given every sign of not wanting her? You didn't contact my daughter after you ran out of here. Not once."

"Would you have wanted me to?"

"Heavens, no!"

"What would you have done if I had?"

"Gotten a court order to keep you away."

In a voice quiet with a common sense that chided, Russ said, "Do you have any idea what that would have done to Cynthia? Or to Diane?" When Gertrude didn't answer, he went on. "I left because I thought it was the best thing for both of them. I stayed away for the same reason. When I contacted Diane six years ago, it was because I felt she was old enough and because I couldn't stay away any longer. She's my daughter. There's no denying that fact."

Gertrude looked as if she did want to deny it but couldn't. Her frustration escaped in subtle ways — the faint compression of her lips, the shift of her fingers, her refusal to blink.

Russ refused to be intimidated by that unremitting stare. "I'm not sure how much she's told you about our relationship. We meet for lunch every few months. We've developed a mutual appreciation. I love hearing about what's going on in her life, she loves hearing about what's happening in mine. Do you know where I live?"

A muscle in her cheek moved. It could have been either a twitch or a gesture of dismissal. "She told me you lived at a school in Connecticut."

"Did she tell you that I'm the headmaster of that school? I was chosen last year from a pool of three hundred candidates. It's a position of responsibility and prestige."

Gertrude arched a pale brow. "Is there a point to this self-promotion, Mr. Shaw?"

He smiled with the sudden understanding that she was rather harmless — arched brow, starched blouse, thinned lips and all. In a softer voice he said, "It's Dr. Shaw, and indeed there is. I was up for a good part of last night thinking about this visit. I was prepared to spit in your eye —" he held up a hand "— not a terribly learned expression from a learned man, but apt. When I left here twenty-five years ago, I hated you. Since then I've come a long way in terms of who I am, what I do and how much money I make. I may not hate you now, but I'm not backing down. I'm here this week because Diane asked me to come. If she hadn't invited me to the wedding, I'd probably have come anyway and stood at the back of the church — just as I stood at the back during her graduation from Radcliffe, though she doesn't know that, and I wish you wouldn't tell her. She'd be upset, which would be pointless, since it's water under the bridge. I want her to be happy. That's all I've ever wanted."

He paused for the briefest of instants, then reached the point of his visit. "She's asked me to give her away at the wedding, and I've accepted. Cynthia just found out. She had already arranged for Ray Bauer to do it, and she wasn't thrilled at first, but she agrees that on Diane's day her wish should be respected. I'd like you to do the same."

The silence in the dining room was abrupt. Russ made no move to break it. He was waiting for Gertrude's consent, and the fact that she didn't instantly offer it neither surprised nor bothered him. Cynthia had mentioned the woman's pride. She would answer him in her own sweet time — which was fine, as long as she gave him the answer he wanted.

He didn't expect the subtle shift of her features, this time not in frustration but in what looked surprisingly like remorse.

"There are people," she began more quietly than before, "who take me to be arrogant and bossy and bigoted, and rightly they should. I can be all of those things when I'm crossed, and some of those things even when I'm not. But whatever I do, I do because I believe it's the best thing." She looked off to the side, keeping her jaw firm to show she wasn't apologizing for anything. "I'll admit that I was a bit cruel cutting Cynthia off without a cent when you two eloped, but I was angry and hurt that she hadn't taken my advice, and I truly believed that only drastic measures would bring her back to me."

"She had a *baby*. You didn't come to see Diane once in those three months."

"Four months," Gertrude corrected, looking him in the eye now. "Cynthia stayed in that apartment for a whole month after you left, waiting for you to return, and she mourned you in earnest for months after. I'd be less than honest if I said that didn't bother me."

"You hated me that much?"

"I loved Cynthia that much. She was my only child, and she was heartbroken."

"But you weren't ready to go out and bring me back."

"No. I didn't think that would be in her best interest. Matthew was a far better match for her. He gave her the stability you couldn't have provided. But that's not my point. My point is that I love my daughter and don't want to see her unhappy. The same applies to my granddaughter. So. If your giving Diane away at the wedding will make her happy, I won't fight it."

Russ couldn't quite bring himself to thank her, though he did feel immensely relieved. He also felt a glimmer of understanding for the woman. Lips pursed, he reflected on that for a minute before nodding and turning to leave. Beneath the archway, he turned back and in a tentative voice asked, "Just for the record, if Cynthia hadn't called you, would you have gone looking for her?"

Gertrude's chin tipped up again. "I already had, and I'd already seen the baby. I used to sit in a rented car on the edge of the park on weekends and watch while you two handed her back and forth."

Russ's throat tightened. He stared at her, thinking about stubbornness and pride and loss. Then, with another nod, he turned, only to stop again. He didn't look back this time. "One last question. If Cynthia and I were to start seeing each other again, if she were to visit me in Connecticut, would you give her trouble?"

After what seemed an eternity to Russ, Gertrude said, "Cynthia is a grown woman. A widow. I no longer have any control over her."

"She loves you and wants to please you. Would you give her trouble?"

The older woman's voice grew quiet. "Now, that wouldn't be in my best interest, would it?"

He did look back at her then. "What do you mean?"

"I have nothing to hold over Cynthia anymore. She is financially independent and socially secure. She doesn't need me the way she did twenty-five years ago. If she chooses to see you and I object, she's very well apt to defy me again, only this time she wouldn't have any reason to come back. Frankly, I don't care for the thought of being estranged from my only daughter at this point in my life."

The implication of what she was saying boggled Russ's mind. He wanted to make sure he'd heard right. "You wouldn't make life miserable for her?"

"Not on that score." One corner of her mouth moved in what Russ could have sworn was the germ of a smile. "On others, of course, I would. I'm Gertrude Hoffmann. It's in my nature to be demanding and iron-willed, even overbearing at times. The day I can't cause a stir on one matter or another will be the day they put me in the ground. Have you any more questions?"

Russ thought about it, then shook his head. With a final nod and a small wave of farewell, he showed himself to the front door and went out to the car. The day seemed suddenly much brighter.

Chapter Six

The wedding rehearsal went off without a hitch on Thursday evening, and Cynthia couldn't have been more delighted. She was pleased to begin with, having gotten word shortly beforehand that Jimmy Schuler had regained consciousness. Added to that, the bridesmaids and groomsmen — bar one Jared Flynn — had all arrived in St. Louis intact, neither of the flower girls had misbehaved, and her mother hadn't said boo when Russ went through the motions of walking Diane down the central aisle of the church, so Cynthia was feeling good all over.

The feeling got even better as they moved from the church to Granatelli's, Nick's family's restaurant on the Hill, where the rehearsal dinner was to be held. The restaurant was small, but upscale and classy in its way, with white tablecloths, white linen napkins and fresh flowers. Candles on each of the tables, as well as paintings and photographs on the walls, gave it the homey atmosphere that suited Nick's family so well.

Cynthia liked the Granatellis, many of whom she'd met before. She liked Teresa, who, plump but stately, had a natural dignity to rival Gertrude's. She liked Dom, with his white moustache and commanding nose, and Uncle Vito, with the ever-present cigar that smelled up the place but looked so much a part of the man that no one dreamed of complaining. She liked Nick's sisters, Paula, Frankie and Sophia, and his brothers, Carlo and Vinnie — all blond, as was Nick, whom she adored. Mostly she liked the fact that Nick and Diane were in love, and that their love surmounted the differences in background that a generation before had caused such heartache. If Gertrude had any objections to the match, she hadn't dared say so to Cynthia. She must have known Cynthia would fight tooth and nail for her daughter's right to happiness.

So Cynthia was feeling good about that, too. And then there was Russ, who had hardly left her side since they'd arrived at the restaurant. She enjoyed having him there. She enjoyed introducing him to Nick's family, enjoyed the way he fitted into the group, enjoyed the way he held his own in conversation. She enjoyed the way he stood with an arm or a shoulder brushing hers, the way he brought her a drink from the bar, put a hand at her waist to guide her to a table, pulled out her chair. He was a gentleman, and though she had never found him lacking in that respect years before, this was different. He was socially suave and urbane, more so than she ever could have wished. Twenty-six years before she'd been bowled over by the boy in the soda shop; now she was bowled over by the man that boy had become.

She was sorry when the evening ended. Too soon, Russ drove her home and walked her to her door. Though her senses were keyed up for something warm and exciting — and though the longing look he gave her suggested he wanted it, too — he didn't kiss her. Instead, he offered to come by the next day and give her a hand doing whatever last-minute things had to be done. If for no other reason than to keep him close, she accepted the offer.

The result was heaven and hell at the very same time. Russ was with her while she opened newly arrived gifts with Diane, oversaw the tent and table raising in the yard and made a final run-through of the wedding events with Tammy. He sat patiently while she made calls to various out-of-town guests who were starting to arrive. He drove her to the jeweler's to pick up the bridesmaids' gifts, to the dry cleaner's to pick up things Diane would be taking on her honeymoon, to the hospital to visit Jimmy. He even drove her to the manicurist's, then wandered around outside until she was done.

Though he was a joy to be with — calm,

accommodating and patient — his presence was a torment. He touched her, but never for long enough. He looked at her with desire, but never acted it out. He spoke in the low, intimate tone lovers used, the kind that stroked her inside and out, then took a step back while she reeled. By late afternoon she wasn't sure whether the shakiness she felt inside was mother-of-the-bride jitters or pure lust.

Russ had barely brought her back to the house when the phone started ringing again. Whispering asides to him about who each of the calls was from, she talked with a cousin who had arrived with her family from Cleveland, a former business associate of Matthew's who was in with his wife from Denver, a friend of Gertrude's whom Cynthia had known forever. Then Diane called from Nick's, reporting that people were gathering at the Granatellis' and asking if they would be along soon. It was a perfect solution to Cynthia's problem. She could be with Russ, yet safe. The more people around, the more diffused her awareness of him would be.

That didn't turn out to be the case. The party at the Granatellis' was wonderful, but not once did Cynthia forget the man by her side. They talked together, moved together, laughed together every bit as naturally as when they'd been kids. Likewise, there were times when the party receded and they were alone, sharing a thought or a story or a reaction to something another person said as though they were the only ones in the room.

That happened increasingly as the evening went on. By eleven, Russ was feeling a distinct need to be alone with Cynthia, if only for a short time. Leaning close, he said, "Are you tired?"

She knew she should be. She knew she should go home to bed, given the eventful day that was ahead. But her senses were humming. She was more awake than she'd been in years. "I don't think I could sleep if I tried."

"Want to go for a ride?"

"I'd love to."

"Think anyone will miss us?"

She glanced around. The party was still in full swing. "Are you kidding?" Slipping a hand in his, she led him through the crowd to where Diane was laughing with a group of friends. "We're taking off, sweetheart. Shall I see you back home?"

"Sooner or later — probably later. Better still, don't wait up, Mom, okay? I'll be more relaxed that way. And I'll have everyone be quiet when we get back so we don't wake you up."

Cynthia touched her hair. She couldn't quite believe her baby was getting married in the morning. Then again, given the work she'd done planning the wedding, she could believe it quite well. "Don't forget, Franco and his crew are coming to do hair at ten. Pass the word."

Diane smiled. "I already have." She kissed Cynthia, then Russ. "See you tomorrow."

The air outside was hot and still. Russ didn't have to be told that a storm was coming on. Anyone could tell, what with the humidity and the dark, starless sky — even a person whose own senses had been storming for hours. His blood was hotter than the air, his arousal heavier than the humidity, and as for the darkness of the sky, that was the way he felt when he thought of leaving on Sunday. There was so much yet to be said, so much to be done. *So much.*

After tucking Cynthia into the car, he went to the driver's side and slid in behind the wheel, but he didn't turn on the ignition. Instead, he caught up her hand and brought it to his mouth.

"I don't want to go for a ride," he breathed against it. "Not really."

She was looking at him, sure that if she didn't kiss him soon she would die. "Me, neither. Russ?"

He rubbed her knuckles against his mouth. "I love you so much."

"Oh, God," she whispered, and opened her hand. She traced his lips for a minute, parted them and leaned over the gearshift to meet him halfway. Their mouths touched and fused, and it was as though twenty-five years of separation had never been. The fire, the balm, the bliss were so intense that by the time they parted for a breath, there were tears in her eyes.

"Can we go somewhere?" he whispered hoarsely.

"Please," she whispered back. "Quickly."

He drove one-handed. The other hand was wrapped in both of hers, anchored against her throat. Her eyes were on his face. He caught her gaze as often as he dared take his from the road. It was brilliant with excitement and need, both of which shone through the thick, dark night. Once, then a second time, he hastily pulled to the side of the road to kiss her again, and if his kisses held more raw need than finesse, he knew she understood. He could taste the hunger in her mouth, could feel the desire that set her slender body to shaking.

By the time they arrived at the inn, large drops of rain had begun to splatter the windshield. Leaving the doorman with a ten-dollar bill to park the car, Russ grabbed Cynthia's hand and ran inside. They took the stairs, moving as quickly as Cynthia's heels would allow, and when that wasn't fast enough, she slipped the shoes off and ran faster.

He fumbled with the door, finally unlocked it and pushed it open. The bed had been neatly turned back in his absence and a low light left on, but he barely noticed. As the door clicked shut behind them, he slid his fingers into her hair, covered her mouth with his and gave her a frantic kiss that spread to her cheeks, then her eyes.

"I can't believe you're here," he whispered.

"I'm here." She was unbuttoning his shirt, desperate to touch him. In a fluid motion that pushed the cotton fabric aside, she slid her palms over his chest and ribs to his waist. In the next breath, she put her mouth where her hands had touched.

Russ was in heaven. He braced shaky arms against the door on either side of her and bent his head over hers. "Sweetheart . . . sweetheart . . . what you do to me."

"I love you, Russ," she said, raising her face. Her mouth met his again, and this time, while their lips continued to nip and suck, they went at their clothes. Cynthia's halter dress fell to the floor not far from Russ's shirt and slacks. He released her bra and filled his hands with her breasts, while she pushed his shorts over his hips.

"Hurry," she cried, straining closer, frantic with need.

No less frantic himself, Russ kicked off his shorts, scooped her up and carried her to the bed. He set her down on her knees in the middle of it and, with timeout to touch all he bared, freed her of her silk panties. While they knelt facing each other, breathing harder than if they'd just come off a long run, he reached for the pins in her hair.

"I want this all over me. I've dreamed of it. It's so beautiful."

She helped him with the pins, helped him comb through her hair with his fingers until it flowed softly over her shoulders. Then, draping her elbows over his shoulders, she gave him her mouth. At the same time, he brought her body tightly against his, drew her thighs over his and entered her.

Her cry was muffled in his mouth. Seconds later, her back hit the bed and he began to love her inside with long, hot strokes. She wanted to savor them and everything else about his body, but the intensity was too great. Within minutes she erupted into a climax so powerful and prolonged that she was never to know where one orgasm ended and the next began.

For Russ, too, the pleasure went on and on. The memory of their lovemaking, which had kept him hard night after night for years, was nothing compared to the heat of the present. His body was slick with sweat by the time he finally let his weight go on her. He rolled to the side and drew her to him, tightening his arms when, still shaken by inner spasms, she began to cry.

"What, sweetheart? What is it?" But he knew even before she told him. He was feeling the same overwhelming emotion.

"I've missed you so much," she gulped through huge tears that wet his throat. "Part of me has been gone —"

"— gone all this time." His arms tightened until he feared he would crush her. His head was bent over hers, his breath was urgent against her temple. "There was always that empty spot. I kept thinking it would fill in —"

"— but it never did. I tried to put other things there, like Matthew and my friends and my causes —"

"— and my students and my courses, but it didn't work. There was always that void, and it hurt —"

"— so *much.*"

"Ahhh, sweetheart," he whispered, moving his head as he kissed her until he could reach her mouth again, "I love you, Cyn . . . love you, sweetheart." He rolled her over, then over again, kissing her all the while. Ending on top, he began to make love to her again, moving down her body, touching and tasting all the places he had missed for so long.

She writhed beneath him until she could take no more. "Now, Russ, *now.*"

Hard and heavy with need, he surged into her, then proceeded to make up for the time they had lost by loving her until she came again — only to realize that wasn't enough. He climaxed, but still he wanted her. The sounds she made, the touch of her hands and the motions of her body told him she felt the same.

They made love long into the night. Hours had passed before either of them was ready to settle onto the damp and rumpled sheets for long, and then it wasn't with exhaustion but with gales of breathless laughter that only two people who are pleased with themselves and in love with each other can produce.

"You haven't changed, Russell Shaw," she hummed against his shoulder. "You're as insatiable as ever."

He spread a hand over her backside to mold her closer. "Look who's talking. I haven't had a workout like this in years."

"How many years?"

"Twenty-five."

"Mmm. That's good."

"And you? Did you drive Matthew wild like you do me?"

"It was different with Matthew. Pleasant, but sedate. There were never grounds for comparison."

"Mmm. That's good."

"But he was a fine man, Russ. He was kind. He loved me, and he loved Diane. I tried to be a good wife to him."

"From everything I've read and heard, you were."

She sighed. "But did I love him? Ahhh, there's the question. I tried to, but it never came close to the kind of all-consuming love

I had with you." She tipped her head back and looked over the plane of his lean cheek to his eyes. "I prayed I'd never see you. I went out of my way over the years not to know what you were doing with your life. I never quite trusted that I wouldn't want to run off to be with you — or that you wouldn't turn and walk away from me again." Her eyes misted and her voice fell to a plaintive whimper. "You won't do that, Russ, will you?"

He brought her over on top of him. "No, love." He kissed her eyes. "I couldn't."

"It would kill me."

"It would kill me, too."

"So what are we going to do? You're leaving Sunday."

"Only if you can't find room for me in your house."

Her heart soared. "You'll stay?"

"Why not?"

"What about school?"

"I'm on summer vacation."

"You have the whole summer off?" Her mind leaped at the possibilities.

"Yes and no."

"What does that mean?" She held her breath.

"I'm due in England on the fifth of July. I'm committed to spending the summer in Oxford collaborating with a don there on a book on education."

She continued to hold her breath.

"Want to come with me?" he asked, and started to smile just as she did because he knew very well what her answer would be.

"I'd love to."

"I'll be busy. Writing a book takes time and concentration."

"That's okay. I'll catch up on all the reading I haven't been able to do this spring, and write letters and take walks."

"I was planning to rent a house in the Cotswolds. Does that sound okay?"

She grinned. "I think I could live with it."

"Then, when I'm done, I thought I'd spend a few days in London, and maybe drive north to Scotland for a few more. Would that be a problem?"

"Are you kidding?"

"I have to be back before Labor Day," he cautioned. "School doesn't begin until a week later, but there'll be plenty to do before then."

She rested her chin on his chest. "What's it like, your place at Hollings?"

"It's a Tudor, wood and brick, with a grape arbor and an old-fashioned well and lots of trees." He ran his fingers through her hair, spreading it around her. "You'll like it, Cyn. It's on campus but set apart so that there's plenty of privacy. It's the kind of house we used to talk about having one day. I mean, it's not as grand as yours —"

She put her hand over his mouth. "I don't care about grand. I care about *you*. You could live in a shack on the tundra and I'd follow you there. That's what I was trying to tell you Monday night. It's one of the reasons I was so crushed when you left me. I've had wealth, and, yes, it makes life easier. But it isn't worth diddly if I can't have you. Don't put me through that misery again, Russ. Don't ever, ever, *ever* do it."

Grasping her waist, he raised her just enough for a kiss. He was about to tell her that he wouldn't ever, ever, *ever* leave her again, when the kiss heated and spread, and before he could contain the flame, she was beneath him and he was inside her again.

It was a while later before he said the words, and by that time they were both so drowsy that the words were slurred. But Cynthia heard them, and held them to her heart as she fell asleep in his arms. Just to make sure she knew he meant them, he repeated them several hours later, when, with dawn sending shards of pale color over the Frontenac treetops, he drove her home.

It was a gem of a day, sunny and dry after the rain the night before. The rich alto of the organ filled the air. With rosebuds in soft shades of cream, pink and peach on the pews and on arbors framing the altar, the church looked beautiful, as did the guests, who filled

131

row after row, waiting expectantly for the processional to begin.

Cynthia, too, waited, her heart beating fast beneath the corsage that had been carefully pinned to her dusty pink gown. She had just been escorted down the aisle and now stood beside Gertrude, who looked surprisingly soft in dove gray. At a change in the music, she turned to watch the groomsmen enter. They were a handsome group. She smiled at each one whose eye she caught, but her attention inevitably returned to the rear of the church. The bridesmaids appeared one by one, looking as exquisite as she had intended in shades of peach, dusty rose and gray. The maid of honor passed as planned, then the flower girls, leaving soft pink petals in their wake.

The music changed again, and this time when Cynthia looked back, her breath caught in her throat. The two people she loved most in the world were there — Diane, looking more stunning than any bride had ever been in her gown of satin and beaded lace, with her cascading bouquet and the headpiece of flowers and veiling, that barely hid the glittering tear-shaped diamond earrings her father had given her that morning; and Russ, looking more handsome than any father of the bride had ever been with his white standing collar, his pale gray cutaway coat and trousers, his cream-colored boutonniere.

Tears came to her eyes as she watched them slowly approach. When she brushed them away, new ones simply took their place. She smiled through them as she caught Diane's eye, and when she found Russ looking at her, her smile grew even softer. He was a beautiful man inside and out, with a beautiful daughter who had been the focus of her passion for the twenty-five years he'd been gone from her life. Now he was back, and the passion would broaden and shift. She felt she was the luckiest woman in the world.

Russ must have read that in her eyes, because his own spoke of sheer adoration in the brief minute before he passed. As she faced front, Nick was approaching the foot of the altar. Gently, Russ lifted Diane's veil and kissed her cheek, then placed her hand in Nick's. By the time he had come to stand by Cynthia's side, the bride and groom were in the priest's care.

Cynthia felt Russ's fingers twine with hers. Looking up through her tears, she saw the sparkle of his own, and in that instant understood the precious second chance they'd been given. His fingers tightened possessively, and while Diane and Nick exchanged their vows, silently they did, too.

Their hearts heard every word.

About the Author

Barbara Delinsky was born and raised in suburban Boston. She worked as a researcher, photographer and reporter before turning to writing full-time in 1980. With more than fifty novels to her credit, she is truly one of the shining stars of contemporary romance fiction. This talented writer has received numerous awards and honors, and her involving stories have made her a *New York Times* best-selling author. There are over twelve million copies of her books in print worldwide — a testament to Barbara's universal appeal.

We hope you have enjoyed this Large Print book. Other Thorndike, Wheeler or Chivers Press Large Print books are available at your library or directly from the publishers.

For more information about current and upcoming titles, please call or write, without obligation, to:

Publisher
Thorndike Press
295 Kennedy Memorial Drive
Waterville, ME   04901
Tel. (800) 223-1244

Or visit our Web site at:
www.gale.com/thorndike
www.gale.com/wheeler

OR

Chivers Large Print
published by BBC Audiobooks Ltd
St James House, The Square
Lower Bristol Road
Bath BA2 3SB
England
Tel.   +44(0) 800 136919
email: bbcaudiobooks@bbc.co.uk
www.bbcaudiobooks.co.uk

All our Large Print titles are designed for easy reading, and all our books are made to last.